Mind That 'tis My Brother

The Publishers gratefully acknowledge the support of

The Arts Council / An Chomhairle Ealaíon.

Mind That 'tis My Brother

GAYE SHORTLAND

POOLBEG

Published in 1995 by
Poolbeg Press Ltd,
Knocksedan House,
123 Baldoyle Industrial Estate,
Dublin 13, Ireland

A catalogue record for this book is available from the British Library

ISBN 1 85371 421 6

Cover etching by Nicky Hooper
Cover design by Poolbeg Group Services Ltd
Set by Poolbeg Group Services in Garamond 10/13
Printed by The Guernsey Press Ltd,
Vale, Guernsey, Channel Islands.

A NOTE ON THE AUTHOR

Gaye Shortland was born and brought up in Bantry, Co Cork. When Gaye left school she went to work in the accounts department of Cork corporation. She then saw David Lean's *Lawerence of Arabia* and decided she wanted to chase Nomads. Before going off to chase Nomads she got a first class honours degree in English and Italian and a first class MA. She spent the next eighteen years in Africa chasing Touareg nomads.

She now lives in Cork with her three children. Gaye Shortland has previously had a story short-listed for the Ian St James awards. This is her first novel.

For Pat McGinn, with love and admiration

CHAPTER 1

Me brothur Liam knew I wanted to be cremated an me ashes scattured onta the grave a Little Nelly a Holy God back in the Good Shepherd convent in Cork. So he had me cremated ovur an he brought me home in a bag. In his luggage like, in a shouldur-bag. I thought twas a nice touch, y'know, like Oscar's "A *hand*-bag!" There I was, not born or bred but at any rate dead in a handbag. Yeh never know what to expect, do yeh? At any stage.

Yeh know what they say about Rest in Peace an all that? Shur, tis all bull! I've had nothin but hair-raisin experiences since I died. Like on the boat. There we were, starin at the waves, an Liam lookin nice with the wind blowin at his Luke Perry quiff an he listenin to my Vangelis tape on the Walkman. An I'm on a high because I can hear it too an it sounds grand with the rhythm a the boat –

You ask me where to begin
Am I so lost in my sin?
You ask me where did I fall
I'll say I can't tell you when
But if my spirit is lost
How can I find what is near?
Don't question I'm not alone
Somehow I'll find my way home
– when the next thing I notice a well-heeled fella furthur

along the rail lampin us. Here we go, sez I. Me heart sank
to the bottom a the urun. I don't have to tell yeh I wasn't
in the mood. Liam nevur let on but I could tell by the glint
in his eye that he knew he was onta a good thing. Took
me down to the bar an propped me up agin the countur –
in the urun, in the bag like. An here comes yur man an
starts chattin him up an buyin him pints. Jaysis, I sweated
buckets in the three hours they spent there downin pints
an gropin each othur on the sly. I just knew he'd staggur
off with yur man an leave me there. I had this picture a
meself sloshin around on the bar floor, awash in beer an
vomit. I could've wept. When I thought a the peace an
calm a Little Nellie's grave an the nuns prayin ovur me! An
what if Liam an yur mano went into the jacks for a quickie
an he left me there? Imagine spendin Eternity goin back an
forth ovur the Irish Sea in the jacks a the *St Brendan*! Might
be alright for entertainment value like, come to think of it.

As it happened, when he did staggur off he
rememburred to swing me up on his shouldur but twas my
misfortune that yur mano had a cabin so I spent the night
thrown on the cabin floor instead, listenin to em bonkin
each othur senseless. You can imagine how I felt. I could
smell it – even if I was only ashes.

It reminded me a one time I went on the boats down
the docks in Cork. My name's Tony by the way. Ant'ny, as
we say in Cork. That time, me an Liam went out one night
but we split up when we got inta town. He didn't know at
that stage that I was trawlin so I had to get rid a him.
Liam's a couple a years oldur than me – but I suppose
that'll even itself out now that I'm dead. Or will it? I dunno
– nobody's given me any information at all about the aftur-
life. I'm just blunderin on. Tis like bein alive – like you
dunno what the fuck is goin on or what lies ahead.

Anyway, like I said: Liam an me went inta town an we
split up. There was a ship in an I picked up this sailur

down by the Cats an Dogs – that's the toilets that were down by the Animals' Home. You wouldn't know but the Cats an Dogs was a great place at that time. They've knocked em down since an no wondur. How we worked the toilets – there was a gap in the wall between two of em an yeh could actually function without seein the othur fella at all – through the gap like. Twas a real turn-on. An handy, to say the least. But I didn't do it much, meself. Anyway, this night I picked up the sailur outside the jacks. Struck up a conversation like. "D'yeh come here often?" He said he was from Brazil. Anyway, we went down to the ship an down inta this cabin. There were two bunks an I was in the bottom bunk with yur man. There was anothur pair on the top bunk, havin a great time, the night long – two fellas like. The two sailurs were crackin jokes to each othur on an off in their own language – God only knows what they were sayin. Morning came, an the two sailurs got up, washed, got spick an span, an ran – tore off, right? To do whatevur sailurs havta do when ships are in dock.

So I was lyin there, recuperatin aftur the hard night, an kinda thinkin to meself that the othur fella was still there an he must be asleep. An eventually anyway yur man hung ovur the edge a the bunk an said: "Have yeh a light?" An twas Liam. Me brothur.

"Jaysis Christ! What are you doin heeyur?" sez he.

"Workin me passage to Rio," sez I. "What d'yeh fuckin think I'm doin?"

An up to then, Liam didn't know about me an I didn't know about Liam. About trawlin, I mean. I used to wondur how he always had money. He was workin in a chippur at the time but twas only part-time an it didn't pay that well. If I evur got money I had to hide it an spend it very slowly, especially in the early days because I was scared a me mothur – if she saw me with a lot a dosh she'd be suspicious. I was still at school like. So was Liam but she nevur noticed with him on accounta the job.

Anyway, that was years ago. Golden Days, in-the-sunshine-of-our-happy-youth an all that. The best days a me life without a doubt – but then my life didn't last very long. Which is why I got this kinda extension maybe. I dunno. I dunno what's goin on. Like I said, there wasn't any orientation course.

Anyway, twas hair-raisin again comin through Customs off the boat in me urun in the shouldur-bag, clankin away against the bottle a whiskey the langur on the boat had given Liam for services rendured.

"Mind that! Tis me brothur!" says Liam to the Customs man.

"What d'yeh mean tis yer brother? You can't carry a sealed container like that through the Customs! We'll have to open it up! What have yeh got in there?"

Oh, God! I had visions a bein confiscated an endin up in police laboratories bein tested, with fellas grabbin bits a me an rushin into the jacks for a quick snort.

"Tis me brothur," says Liam. "He died a AIDS in London an I had him cremated ovur."

Well! Yeh should have seen how fast yur mano bundled me back an chalked up the bag! EEC regulations, how are yeh!

That wasn't all. The last leg a our journey was the worst. We got inta a Numbur 8 that was crammed to the gills. Liam hadta stay on the front platform with half-a-dozen othur people. He'd only the one bag – he was aftur leavin everythin else behind in London in a friend's flat – he hadn't much heart for packin at the time. He put me down next to his feet an half-leant half-sat on the small partition between the platform an the drivur which meant he had his ass pushed up agin the drivur's left arm. Always hopeful, me brothur Liam. Does okay, too, though he's not much of a lookur – bit scrawny like, not a pick on him at the best a times. Narra face, brown hair in that Luke Perry quiff effort. A few spots. Nothin special. Nice dark-blue eyes though with black lashes. Typical Cork, in othur words, sharp nose an all. I dunno if he'd any luck with the drivur – I couldn't see much from the floor. The way it was, I'd no trouble seein through the bag an the urun but aftur that I hadta have an unobstructed view – don't ask me why. So I dunno if Liam got much joy outa the drivur but I suppose he got off on it anyway because he forgot about me an I got kicked along the floor till I was teeterin on the edge a the step near the door.

The bus climbed the hill up to Mayfield. Mayfield – y'know? Where they tie the childrun to the chairs an go off down to the pub? Where they go out an leave the chip-pan boilin on the gas cookur in the hopes the house'll burn down an they'll be given a transfer to anothur part a the city? Full a knackurs? That's where I grew up. That makes me a North-sidur. An proud of it – chip-pans an all.

"The door's open!" says one a the ten people on the platform. *Do not cross the white line or talk to the driver.*

"Well, what d'ye want now?" asked the drivur. "D'ye want me to go an get anothur bus or d'ye want me to get ye home? Make up yeer minds now! Shur, tis an automatic door! Watch now, twill close again!" An when we swung round the cornur, it did. "Watch again now an twill open!" An he swerved round the next left-hand cornur to demonstrate.

I nearly died. I thought I was gone. I could see meself flyin outa the door an by the time Liam got the drivur's elbow outa his arse an got off the bus I'd be ground inta Summurhill undur the traffic.

"That's all very fine an salty," says a woman sittin on the ledge a the front winda with somebody else's fat baby on hur lap. "But who's goin to pay compo if we fall out? Yurself or Bus Éireann?"

"Yerra, sue away! Tis about time they fixed up their ould buses – c'mere, will I stop an take that ould wan home? Ah, shur, I will – she looks starved!"

He stopped an anothur four people squeezed on with a big fold-up buggy. Off we went again with the starved ould wan hangin onto the bar like a trapeze artist when we swung round cornurs with the door flyin open an shut an me on the edge a the platform with me heart in me mouth.

The drivur had turned up his radio. Now he was on a complete high. That's what powur does to yeh. Or maybe he was gettin off on Liam's arse. Who knows?

"*And I will always love you-ou-ou-ou-ou!*" he screeched with Whitney Houston, cranin his neck to see the side-mirror round the woman an the fat baby. "Keep yeer heads down there or I can't see to get ye up the hill! *Love you-ou-ou-ou-ou-ou!*"

I said a prayur a thanksgivin when we got off that bus – an I was nevur much of a one for religion.

Liam didn't head for home. No, he branched off down the Glen (the Glin, I should say) an inta Dec's house. I was delighted. I wasn't lookin forward to seein me family at all. Twas goin to be a bit grim seein me mothur. But Dec now! Grand! The front door was open so in we went. It isn't a Corporation house – tis one a them small old-fashioned ones on a side-road leadin down to the Glen. There was a grand smell a roast meat comin from the kitchen but there was no sign a anyone there.

"Dec? Dec!" No answur. Up the stairs with us an inta Dec's bedroom. There he was, stretched out in his bed with a big heavy book called *The Decline and Fall of the Vatican* on his chest. He was unconscious. He looked pretty good lyin there bare-skinned – as much as we could see a him. He has that very white skin, very clear with a slight rosy touch to it – this is me gettin poetic now – an a lovely face with a good straight nose an a good shape to his eyebrows an lips, y'know what I mean? And a kinda sweet expression – some a the time anyway. Oh, yeah, an a bit of a cleft to his chin – but very soft. He's heaviur than he used to be – a bit more muscle on him – he used to be very slim an girlish in his teens. His browny-blonde hair was springing off his forehead – it always looked very alive – electric, like Prince or Seal would say. Yeah, that's Dec.

I dunno – I felt very fond a him when I saw him. I'd a loved to be able to give him a hug. I'd a loved to feel his arms around me. In fact, I'd a loved to just slide into the bed with him an put me head on his chest – somethin I'd never really thought a doin while I had all me equipment like. Liam started shakin him an *The Decline and Fall of the Vatican* fell with a thump onta the floor. He woke up with a fierce start.

"Take it easy – tis me! Liam."

"Liam? God . . . you're back . . . yeh gave me an awful fright!" He sat up. "Hold on a sec . . . I'm a bit . . . " Big sigh. "Jay, I was having a grand dream . . . that book." He rubbed a hand across his eyes. "God, you spoilt it all on me . . . I was an Italian Cardinal in bed with his catamite and I just know if you hadn't woke me up I'd have had the climax of my life . . . Shit." He clutched at his stomach an moaned. "Do you know my mothur is trying to starve me to death?"

"Again?"

"Did she tell yeh?"

"Naw, I didn't see hur. She must be after goin ovur to the shop. I came straight up. I'm just off the boat."

"Don't *mention* the word boat t'me! Wasn't I on the boat myself last week! I went as far as Swansea an came back! Wait an I tell yeh . . . "

"Tony's dead. He died last week."

Dec stared an his blue eyes filled with tears. I was touched to see it, I tell yeh. He sat there an let the tears spill down an didn't even wipe em away. After a while he said, with a catch in his voice: "Were you with him at the end?"

"Yeah . . . but he was doped up to the eyeballs."

Dec rubbed a hand across his nose. A big sniff.

"Why didn't yeh send for us? Were there many at the funeral?"

"Oh, I just had him cremated. Quick job. I have him here."

"Jesus! What d'yeh mean?"

"Heeyur! In the bag." He gave the bag a small kick. The jolt that went through me!

"Give us a look!"

Liam pulled the urun out an handed it to him. He turned it round in his hands. Not as good as a hug, but nice.

"Can't we open it? I'd like to see what it looks like."

It!

"I suppose we can."

"Gimme the knife there – no, you do it."

Liam cut the seal round the top a the urun an flipped back the lid. "That's him. That's Tony."

Dec prodded his middle fingur inta me ashes an I swear to God a tremor went through me. Of pleasure, I mean. I know yeh don't believe me. Yeh have yur fixed ideas about the spirit world, right? I was surprised meself, to be honest. Especially since he nevur turned me on when I was in the body – in the flesh, as they say. Just goes to show. Yeh nevur know what to expect.

"*Amazing*," says Dec as if he was a fuckin scientist or somethin. "*Amazing*. To think that this was Tony."

Was Tony, how are yeh!

Dec closed the lid an put me on his bedside table with the rosary beads an the holy pictures an the ould women's prayur-books that he d'be findin in churches. I wondured where he had planked his collection a porn. Next thing he got outa bed an started searchin for his clothes an all of a sudden me heart was in me throat an I was findin it difficult to breathe. A course he had dragged the sheet out aftur him an pulled it up undur his armpits – outa modesty – he'd learned that in *The Girls' Book of Piety* when he was fourteen – but, since he was facin Liam, I had a grandstand view from behind. Twas a very weird sensation – bein turned on when there was nothin to turn on. Jesus, this was confusin! I was supposed to be past all that, wasn't I?

When I next paid attention – like when I dragged my attention away from his ass – he was talkin about his mothur. He adores his mothur. "God forgive hur! The woman's been torturing me! Four days I've been lying there and if you hadn't come now I'dve had anothur twenty-one hours to go." His voice is really lovely – kinda high an clear but strong with a kinda crack to it. "I didn't have a bite to eat since I got off the boat on Thursday!"

"But what were yeh doin on the boat anyway?"

"I'll tell yeh about that in the minute. Where're me boots? I came straight home here on Thursday – course I hadn't the price of a box a matches on me at that stage – I was skint. Home to The Bosom. Some bosom! Refused to feed me. The usual."

"Why didn't yeh go down the docks?" asked Liam. He'dve been off like a shot.

"To be honest with you, I didn't have the energy for it. And I'd seen enough of boats. And I knew if I earned some money, I'd only drink it. I was in that kind of mood. C'mon."

Liam stuffed me back in the bag right inta a bunch a smelly socks an undurwear so I choked me way down the stairs an when I got me breath back Liam was aftur goin ovur to the shop.

I had nothin to lose. I dunno what I wanted. I'd been

really turned on in the bedroom and . . . well, I just wanted his attention. I got it. With knobs on. "Dec! Dec!" I called. "Dec, boy! Come ovur heeyur!" Even I didn't hear meself but it worked anyway. He came ovur where Liam had dumped me, an squattin down he pulled the urun outa the bag. Then he knelt down, an proppin the urun up on his dick – Jaysis! – he flipped the lid back an stuck his fingur in an kinda swirled it around. Then, while I was tryin to get ovur the shock a that, he wet his fingur-tip with his tongue an pressed it inta the ashes. An very slowly he raised the fingur an licked me off. What he thought he was doin I've no idea but I couldn't remembur evur feelin anythin like that before. If I'd had arms an legs an all the rest of it I'd have eaten him alive on the spot. Twas more like a fantasy than anythin that really happens to yeh, y'know what I mean? Twas that intense like.

Then the door banged an he slammed down the lid an shoved me back in the bag. "Deo Gratias!" says he an Liam came in. Chapter 66 a the Benedictine Rule. *If a knock comes at the door the monk is to answer 'Deo Gratias'.* Queer things yeh pick up hangin around Dec. Liam had brought bread an eggs an rashurs. They went into the kitchen an started fryin em. But not before Liam had dragged out the bottle a whiskey yur man on the boat had given him. They took that into the kitchen with em. So I was left there, still hypurventilatin aftur the recent encountur. I thought I might suffocate to death in the urun. I hadta distract meself so I listened hard an found I could hear what they were sayin in the kitchen.

"Why didn't yeh come down at night an raid the fridge?"

"I wouldn't give her the *soot* of it." Very camp. I could imagine the pose that went with that. "Assumpta snuck an apple up to me the night before last – I ate that alright. That's different. Oh, a *hard* woman! Mothur Love, how are yeh! Frau O'Leary. Mind you, she's *right*! She's put up with enough from me! But I was asking myself how did I come to be lying in that lumpy bed being starved to death by my own mothur? That's what my life has come to! I mean I was made for moonlight and roses. And whiskurs on kittens. And another few of my favourite things." Yelps from the kitchen. "But No Cross No Crown, More to Suffur More to Offur, as the Bon Secours say." He picks up all that stuff from workin with nuns, in hospitals and the like. "But to think that if his dick hadn't been such a monstrosity, I could be livin it up in London right now!"

"His dick! Whose dick?" Liam gave a big scairt a laughtur. "What? What are yeh talkin about for Chrissake?"

"Now, now, now! No profanity, if you please. I'll tell yeh about that in the minute – first my most recent ordeal. Hand me ovur the rashurs there. God forgive hur! Frau O'Leary! I could imagine her standing at the foot of the stairs wafting the smell a the roast beef up the stairs to me with a bit a cardboard box! I thought she'd be up the stairs to me in her jackboots any minute waving the meat under my nose. D'ye know what I did? I imagined it was pork and they were trying to force me to eat it."

"I've lost yeh now." The whiskey was gettin to Liam already. I could tell. They were drinkin it fast. I wondured what it would do to Dec on an empty stomach. He was laughin a lot already – his high bright laugh. He really has a laugh that tinkles an gurgles an is full a mirth an all those othur things you read about in books – if yeh go in for Mills an Boon, that is.

"Wasn't I a Jew?"

"Why . . . oh, yeah . . . "

"Then when that didn't work any more, I pretended it was the odour of human flesh from the chimney stacks – five of em – I could see em from my window or I would have seen em if I'd a been able to sit up in my weakened

11

state. Anyway, I had only twenty-one hours to go and my ordeal would be ovur. Twas like thinkin a Heaven! I'd be standin in the dole queue – the hills would be alive with the sound of music! Then straight down to The Long Valley for a pint!" His voice fell. "But that was only fantasy. I couldn't enjoy a pint with the spectre of Frau O'Leary with her jackboots an whip at me elbow. No, I'dve had to come straight home an hand it all ovur to her. The usual, plus twenty quid to make up for the missed week. Oh, a hard woman!"

They came through with plates an things for the table. It struck me suddenly that in spite a the fact that I was enjoyin the smell a the rashurs cookin an the roast, I wasn't a bit hungry. I mean you'dve expected it considerin the othur sensations I was feelin . . . there was somethin odd here.

They were aftur goin back into the kitchen.

"Yerra, they had him doped up to the eyeballs at the end." They were talkin about me. "He was on drugs all the time like, but towards the end they shot him full of em. He didn't know where he was. They warned me he wouldn't know me or anythin. I thought maybe he did though." Silence for a while – apart from clatterin an bangin with the fryin-pan an that. "C'mere! I've this problem about his will."

"He made a will?"

"Yeah. There he was, doped senseless – that Diomorphine stuff or whatevur it's called – when they realised he hadn't made a will. So they reduced the drugs a bit so he could make one. They brought a solicitur in to do it an there was a bit of a dispute because he said twouldn't be legal. That he wasn't in his senses like. Anyway, they asked me an I said go ahead."

"And what happened?"

"He left everythin he had to our Aunty Mamie."

I did *what*! Jesus!

"Who's she when she's at home? I never heard of her!"

"Shur, he hardly knew hur. Some ould cousin a me mothur's. He certainly didn't want to leave anythin to *hur*. But that's what he said when yur man asked him. Aunty Mamie."

"But shur you can dispute that!'

"Yeah. Not that he had much like. But he was supposed to leave it to me. The few quid like. He'd saved a fair bit in that last job he had. Twas a fairly classy restaurant."

They came back with the food an the whiskey an sat themselves down. Sure enough the bottle was half-empty.

Dec suddenly started laughin his head off. "Where there's a will there's a way!"

Liam spluttured his whiskey ovur the plastic tablecloth. "Jaysis, you're fuckin right! Where there's a will there's a way! We'll do away with the will . . . " Liam was convulsed.

I didn't think twas *that* funny – but then I wasn't half-langurs.

"What's goin on here?" Twas Mrs O'Leary, back from wherevur, in hur apron. "What're ye laughin at like that?"

"Tony's dead!" spluttured Dec.

An the two of em fell all ovur the table laughin their hearts out – bent double!

Well, this is fuckin great, I thought.

"Lord preserve us from all harm!" An there was a small shake to hur voice. "Is that somethin to laugh about? Poor Tony! Have ye no hearts?"

"He's cremated," screamed me brothur, drinking his tears, an he fished me outa the bag.

"Sacred Heart a Jesus!" She took me from him an turned me round in her hands, like Dec had done. Then she looked round as if she was wonderin where to put me – I was an unusual household item. I coulda kissed hur – she looked so hurt an concerned an she put me down so gently – next to the nightlight undur the picture a the

Sacred Heart. She even kinda arranged me in a bettur position, closur to the light, an stood there lookin at me.

A bit a incense would be nice, I thought.

I wished – not for the first time – that I could read people's thoughts. You'd expect a spirit to be able to, wouldn't yeh? But no. I watched her watchin me. She was lookin good, her bottle-blonde hair freshly styled – short, in soft layurs with a big sweep across the front. I wondured where she was aftur havin it done. She has Dec's clear blue eyes an a pretty face, roundur than his. She'd put on more weight, though, an The Bosom as Dec calls it was more impressive than evur. Aftur a while she gave a sigh an turned back to the lads.

"When're yeh goin back, Liam?"

"I dunno. I'll be around for a while anyway . . . "

Anothur sigh. "Twill be lonely ovur without Tony . . . "

"Yeah . . . "

Another sigh an she went out into the kitchen.

"*Oh, the path was deep an wide from footsteps leadin to our cabin,*" sang me brothur, noddin at the night-light with its red dome. "*Above the door there burned a scarlet lamp . . .* "

"C'mere!" She was back at the kitchen door. "Could ye tell me! Why are ye eatin rashurs an eggs an me with a roast in the oven?"

Declan threw hur what I've heard him call "a withering look". He has that to a fine art.

"We're fine, Mrs Leary," says Liam. "This is grand."

She gave a little shrug an was gone again.

"Wouldn't give hur the soot of it!" muttered Dec but loud enough so she probably heard.

"I'm dyin for a cuppa an a fag!" she called out.

Liam sniggured. "I useta say that all the time ovur. You'd be wonderin why they were lookin at yeh queer. But c'mere – tell us about the boat an yur man with the dick!"

"I can't now. She'll hear," muttured Dec.

"She's gone out back. To the line. No – for the coal." Liam could see into the back yard through the winda by rockin back on his chair. "G'wan – tell us quick."

"I can't tell yeh quick! Tis a long story. Well, alright so – I misewell start. I was out bevying with Liz in Loafurs an we met that winda-dressur from En Vogue – d'yeh know him? Oh a *queen* to his backbone! Anyway, he had a friend with him – gorgeous, very dark – and I fancied him at first sight. It turned out his fathur was foreign – from Estonia or some place. We went on to Sir Henry's an we kissed overright straight people an we danced. This is love, says I to myself. We ended up going back to Liz's place – hur folk were away."

Liz is his great friend. Not a fag-hag like – he doesn't go in for paradin around with women an she wouldn't be the type at all anyway. They really are great friends.

"So says I to him when we got there and had the cup a coffee like: 'Would you like to stay?' and he said he would. So Liz's bed was put to use. An it was all very pleasant and what-have-you but the problem was there was nothing I could do with his – appendage. It was *monstrous*!" Dec's lovely voice was cracklin between indignation an laughtur. "It was *huge*. I've nevur seen anything as big, except maybe in a blue movie. Really. Frightening. It was *long* and *thick*."

"So what was the problem?" Liam's mouth was open.

"What was the problem? I could do nothing with it! I mean all I could do was jerk him off. And actually that got too much for me so he had to do it himself like. It was mammoth! He was embarrassed. Lord preserve us from all harm, sez I, you're going to kill me with that! I'll nevur walk again! I mean I don't want a tonsillectomy!" Liam burst out laughin. I had to laugh meself but I wasn't too happy with this yarn. "All he could do was put it between my legs. Friction, like."

In came Mrs Leary with hur tea so they shut up. She sat down an pulled a packet a fags outa hur apron-pocket. Then she stared ovur at me with a fag between hur lips.

"Poor Tony, God help him," says she an she heaved anothur big sigh. "To think a him in that little canistur without a propur funural or a bit . . . " She lit up an sighed again. Then she thought a Liam. She gave him a fag. Dec has nevur smoked. "I remembur him here in this very room – two years ago it was – d'yeh remembur, Dec? Majella was here an ye were dancin with the baby in yeer arms to put him to sleep. You had your record a Gracie Fields' last concert on . . . " She began to sing softly. *"Little old lady passing by, catching everyone's eye, you're a perfect picture in your lavender and lace . . . "*

"And – *twas on the Isle of Capri that I found her,*" sang Dec. So he remembured. That day! All we laughed!

"What are yeh goin to do with that now?" She nodded towards me an me red lamp. "Are yeh goin to give it to yur mothur?"

"God, she wouldn't want it, Mrs Leary. She doesn't hold with cremation. An Tony, well, he wanted to be scattured up on Little Nellie's grave. I dunno if we can do that but that's what he wanted."

"God help us. Poor Tony! The craytur!" She started rubbin hur eyes with the heel of hur hand – the one with the cigarette.

Dec began clearin the table. "Aren't yeh going to eat yer dinnur, Mam?"

"I don't feel like it. I'd better wait for Assumpta anyway. I don't know where she's aftur gettin to."

"Well, if I was you I'd eat me dinnur an when she comes in I'd tell her the kitchen's closed for the day." He would, too. He'd often refused me a cup a coffee late at night because the kitchen was closed since nine o'clock.

This was somethin he'd got from workin in hospitals an monasteries – the communal life, y'know.

"Imagine what she'd have to say to that!"

"Well, what d'yeh have the back a yer hand for?"

Ten minutes latur they were ready to head off. I was almost sorry to leave the mantelpiece. I felt nice an secure an peaceful there. But then I thought a Assumpta comin in an grindin out hur cigarette-butts in me an I felt like a goose was aftur walkin ovur me grave.

We walked inta town. Dec always vamps, even when he has money. I dunno whethur tis to be keepin his figure or whethur he d'be doin penance or what. You nevur know with Dec. When he was fourteen he useta wear a rope tight around his waist like Matt Talbot (one a our saints, an alcoholic or somethin that took to religion). Dec was inta all that sorta thing.

"Well, we got ovur it – carried on like. But no way could I get used to it!" Dec was talkin about Big Dick again. This was killin me. Jealous, I was! I gritted me teeth an listened hard. "I couldn't take it! I might as well have been a virgin like! And you know I'm not into this anal stuff anyway. I mean it isn't so long since I useta have difficulty with a fingur! But even orally I could barely manage – like licking an ice cream – I mean I couldn't take it in my mouth eithur. But despite all that, it was Love's Young Dream alright. He adored the ground I walked on. We snogged all ovur Cork city. Tis a wondur we weren't arrested."

We'd reached Luke's Cross.

"*Regeeeenaaa! Leeeem!*" Someone was screechin from across the road.

"Lawsy me, tis Missy Scarlett!" said Dec. "Don't bother me an don't call me sugah!"

Tizzy was teeterin on the edge a the footpath across the road outside Henchy's pub.

"*Regeeeenaa!*" Regina – that's Dec's nickname.

"Jesus, wouldn't he disgrace yeh?" said Dec. "Tis bad enough being associated with *that* without him screeching *Regina* all over the place. Dat Scarlett – she jes white trash! Ain't got no more manners thun a field-hand!" He looked about him with his chin thrown back. Very camp. Kinda swivellin on the ball of his foot. Then he looked down to about waist-level. "Oh, hello, Mrs Burke!

A small little ould wan had come dodderin outa the shop behind us – or maybe twas outa Ladbrokes (the bookie's) – I didn't notice. I recognised hur – she's a neighour a Dec's. She was wearin slippurs an an oul grey cardigan ovur hur apron. Hur scrap a hair was bright puce. That wasn't a Peter Mark's job! Who in Jesus's name was after doin it at all?

"I'm like a young wan! I'm down in me slippurs," says she in the real high thin Cork voice, grabbin onta Dec's arm in the height a flirtation. If yeh've nevur heard the Cork accent tis hard to describe it but I'll do me best: like every sentence begins high an ends up highur – ends way up in the clouds in a long drawn-out note an in between the beginnin an the end it kinda swoops up and down. Somebody ovur once said to me that Cork people don't talk – they sing – an I kinda know what he meant.

"Leeeeeem!" Now Tizzy was stuck at the toll-booth in the centur a the cross.

Dec threw him one a his witherin looks an turned his back on him. "Mrs Burke, shur you're looking grand! Is that a new cardigan you're wearing?"

"Is it jokin me yeh are? Tis just an oul thing I threw on me. Jacinta gave it t'me – it shrunk in the wash for hur. Mam, sez she, twill do yeh for goin out to the line. I shouldn'tve come out in it at all!" She was still swingin outa his arm. "Shur weren't the shawls a grand thing long go? All me mothur God-rest-hur had to do was throw the oul shawl around hur an it covured a multitude. An shur, yeh nevur had to wash um. But c'mere, isn't there grand dryin these days? We don't know ourselves!"

"Ah, shur, we'll pay for it next month, Mrs Burke. April showurs – with a vengeance," said Dec.

"D'yeh think we'll get a summur this year? Shur, last year we'd no summur at all!"

There was a break in the traffic. Tizzy came sashayin across the road. I dunno what that means exactly – sashayin – but tis somethin Scarlett O'Hara used to do an it sounds grand an it suits him. "Hello, Liam, how's it hangin?" He was beamin all over his face an claspin his hands in that way he has. "When are yeh goin back?"

"I dunno," mumbled Liam, shovin his hands in his jacket pockets an shiftin from foot to foot. I knew he didn't want to be asked about me in fronta the ould wan.

"Did yeh hear about Regina goin all de way to Swansea an turnin back without gettin off de boat?" asked Tizzy.

"She was just givin me a blow by blow account," said Liam. He winked at Tizzy an pulled a face.

Mrs Burke started to shake Dec by the arm, lookin up inta his face through hur lashes, what was left of em.

"Thirty pounds," says she.

Dec stared.

"Thirty pounds."

"Is that so?" He hadn't a clue.

"Is it alright?" she asked, vexed.

"Oh, tis fine . . . but thirty pounds . . . "

"D'yeh think I was an eejit so?"

"Ah, no, Mrs Burke . . . shur you only live once . . . " Then his face cleared. "An it suits yeh."

"Is it too long at the back?" She turned hur head. They were talkin about hur hair.

"Not at all! An the colour is lovely!"

"Yeh wouldn't know when yeh're on yur own – yeh

wouldn't have anyone to tell yeh . . . "

"Well, tis lovely, Mrs Burke. For a change."

"I nearly had a seizure when she told me. Thirty pounds! An shur, it doesn't last kissin time."

"Not interruptin yeh now but are yeh comin, Dec?" asked Liam.

"Who's that little cafflur?" asked Mrs Burke in a loud whispur.

"Don't you know Liam, Mrs Burke? Shur isn't he always up at home? We're off down doing Pana."

"Have ye nothin bettur t'be doin than traipsin up an down Patrick Street? Gallivantin! An, shur, Declan, you're a sore disappointment to us." She let go a Dec an grabbed hold a Liam. "He was a lovely boy – we always said he'd be a priest." Liam giggled an Tizzy let out a kinda whinny. Mrs Burke didn't seem to notice.

"Well, you say a little prayer for me, Mrs Burke," said Declan. "Don't forget me now!" Dec has a way a sayin these things as if he means em. But I suppose he does.

"Forget yeh?" Hur voice rose sky-high. "Shur, I'd nevur forget you, Dec! Didn't I say it to yur mothur the othur day? Mrs Leary, I sez sez I, the novena to St Ant'ny will be comin up soon an this year I'll do it for Dec's intentions, I sez sez I."

"Dec, d'yeh want us to go on without yeh?" Liam an Tizzy were fed up with all this. I dunno, I was enjoyin listenin. But then, I was dead. I had nothin bettur to be doin.

"I'll have to flake away," says Tizzy. "I've a jag tonight." An he clasped his hands.

"Will ye hold on for a minute!" Dec was annoyed. "Mrs Burke, I hate to say this now but don't go *near* Anthony for me. As far as I'm concerned, he's a right chansur. He's alright for finding lost property an that – I'd be the last to say othurwise – I mean where would we be without him?

But pray for something else an the next thing yeh know he pulls a fast one on yeh. No, don't go *near* Anthony – not for me – "

Liam grabbed hold a Dec's arm an started draggin him away.

"But the Mothur of Good Counsel now, or Rita – "

"Will yeh c'*maan*," muttered Liam. "So long, Mrs Burke!"

Tizzy took Dec's othur arm an they rushed him off down Summurhill.

"I'm ill, I'm ill, cried Dame Veronica," says Dec to the sky – or I should say "cried Declan to the sky". I haven't got the hang a this writin stuff yet. I wish I'd been inta readin them Mills an Boons.

"Indeed but you do look a mite wan, my dear." This was Dec again in a different voice. "Do you wish to borrow my cloved orange for a space?"

Liam an Tizzy looked at each othur across Dec. We all knew who Dame Veronica was – an abbess from that book he was crazy about, In the House a Somethinorothur. But who was yur wan with the cloved (*cloved*?) orange? It could be anyone – probably Marie Antoinette or the like – she sounded sorta regal – but we all knew if this was a new craze he'd drive us all spare with it if we let him. When he got started on that sorta thing he didn't know when to stop. I've known him to be anothur person for an entire weekend.

"What about yur man with the big dick?" said Liam, tryin to distract him.

Not a hope.

"Big Dick? But he has not been presented!" Dec stopped. He threw off their arms an started throwin shapes. "We have not had the pleasure! Where is our maid-of-honour?" He beckoned to some poor unfortunate across the road who scuttled away fast. "Jeanne! Jeanne! Come here, girl!"

"Dec!"

But Dec was on a roll. "Ah – so this is Big Dick! But I know the gentleman! Alas, has he lost his manhood? He left it with me? Horrors! Have I perchance mislaid it? Girl!" To Tizzy. "Check my comfit-box."

Tizzy kinda half-turned like he was goin to check a real comfit-box before he stopped himself. Then he blushed.

Tizzy's an ole dote. He's young, nineteen, an very effeminate. But not put-on effeminate. Really effeminate. I mean the likes a some a the lads could get away with bein fine men if they liked – I mean they'd have the physique an all that but Tizzy has only the one ball an it gets told everyone like. He was born that way an it's been the subject a jokes all his life. He thinks he's Scarlett O'Hara half the time – but I mean if he wrapped himself around a pole he wouldn't come out lookin like Vivien Leigh – except in so far as he has narra shouldurs an a girl's ass on him. But he has very thick silky light-brown hair (honey highlights) in a kinda puddin-basin style that he gets done in the salon where he works – a real professional job. Whoevur done his hair put his soul – or his balls – into the job. By the way, I'd a liked to be a hairdressur meself – dunno why I nevur done it when I was young. I was savin up with somethin like that in mind when I . . . well, when I . . . when I *died*? Or should I say when I passed away or crossed ovur? Twas more like a breakthrough than a crossovur. Have I gone alternative now or have I gone mainstream?

Jesus – I was tellin yeh about Tizzy! Call here to me when I forget meself like that! What else about him? Paleish except when he's blushin which is mosta the time. Nice mouth. Really nice mouth. *Gorgeous* mouth actually. Those kinda lips you'd almost lean ovur an take a bite outa. Yeah, that's Tizzy. An oh yeah – the nails bitten off him – he does that when he's at the flicks which is like every day an when he goes too far he hasta wear false nails at work an that's the bane a his life.

He did a bit a Vivien now, partin his lips an smilin up through his eyelashes. "I'm dyin to hear de rest a de story, Dec."

Dec turned on him an grabbed him by the chin. "My child, but you do look winsome today!" An poor Tizzy got the fright of his life when next minute Dec started castigatin him. "Now you take dat Southern Belle simpah off your face listen heah to me! You's jes white trash! Oh, yes'm, you is! Screechin cross de street an callin me Regina in public! De nex time you do dat I'se gonna take a buggy-whip to your hide! What do you tink, Mistah Butlah?"

Liam knew his *Gone with the Wind*. The chin went up an the eyes went narra. "In my opinion a good lashin with a buggy-whip to the tune of Dixie would benefit her immensely!" An he tapped his cigar.

"I'm sorry, Dec," says Tizzy.

"Well, in futyah you jes remembah you's a lady." An with that he swung round an was off down the hill again. "Right. Where was I?" Back on course.

"Love's Young Dream," said Liam.

"Right. As I said, we got ovur it, the difficulty, carried on like. He kept apologising. But he liked a kiss and a cuddle which is what I like myself. Anyway, he asked me to go to London with him – which is where he works. So, said goodbye to everyone. Got on the boat. Then, a bad start. I was terribly sad at leaving home and tremendously excited at the same time. So I wanted to go down to the bar and have a sing-song – you know! He wanted a cup of tea. I had no money at all. So we had tea. Then I noticed he had a face on him. There's a few things I want to say to you, says he. Right, says I. You get on far too well with women, says he, it makes me feel it's their company you want, not mine. I want you to stop that. No problem, says I. Grand, says I. What could I say though? What could I say? I had no money. I was totally dependent on him."

Four big eyes, all sympathy, were fixed on Dec. I was havin trouble sortin out me own feelins.

"Another thing is, I want to look as young as I can for as long as I can. So I like to wear make-up, says he. No problem, says I. You wear what you like! Grand, says I. But you know me now! I like a man to be a man. If I wanted make-up I would seek a woman to be made-up. But what could I say? He owned me at this point. Next thing: he was a vegetarian and I had to be too. All this an we passing Blackrock Castle. I mean if I could swim, which I can't, I'd a jumped in an swum ovur to Mahon."

It wouldn'ta been the first time he'd jumped in the rivur. Nor the last, I'd say. He was always at it. Always at low tide. So far.

We were standin outside the Garda Station on MacCurtain Street at this point. Not that we'd any intention a goin in. No, our club happens to be across the street from the Gardaí, upstairs ovur a disused place that looks like a garage underneath, an right next door to Whippins an Lashins (that's The Irish Girl Guides to you) on one side an *The Irish Times* office on the othur. Very respectable, we were. They were goin to call into the club but Liam an Tizzy were all agog an wanted Dec to go on with the yarn.

"C'man an we do Pana!" said Tizzy.

"I thought yeh'd a jag?" said Liam.

"Dat's latur."

"But are you not going to *The Crying Game*?" asked Dec. "No? I'm *amazed*."

"I'm going tommora."

"How many times have you seen it now?"

"Twelve times, I tink."

"God, you're totally lampy! But could I ask you a question?"

"What? Ask away."

"How long is it since you've been to Mass? I mean where is Our Lady in your life, I'd like to know?"

"C'mere, though," said me brothur, ignorin Dec. "Who are yeh meetin latur?" The thing about me brothur is: he shoulda been a reportur. He missed his vocation.

"A fella down from Dublin."

"Chalk it down! Chalk it down!" said Liam, stretchin out the arm. "Tizzy has a real *date* tonight!"

"You mean you're not goin down the docks to get beaten up?" asked Dec. "No? I'm *amazed*."

"Met him last night. Works on RTE." Tizzy was tryin to look modest an ended up lookin smug like the cat that got the cream.

"*What!* You're into the Big Time an yeh didn't even tell us!" This was Dec. "Oh, you're the fly boy! Next thing you'll be gettin a job outa him. They'll give yeh your own spot on Zig an Zag: Tizzy on The Den."

"He's nuthin to do with De Den!"

"Yeh might get to shag Dustin," says Liam. Dustin is a kinda vulture in case yeh're not a Den fan. "Live."

"Tizzy mightn't be up to that, Liam," says Dec.

"I tell ye, he's nuthin to do with De Den," says poor Tizzy, gettin excited.

"No? Well, Bosco then." Dec started doin the puppet's high voice. "*I'm a good boy, amn't I?*"

"He's nuthin to do with Bosco eithur!" Tizzy was gettin upset. His face was all flushed.

"I'm *amazed*," said Dec, steppin back two paces. "I mean, are you *sure*?"

C'mere! I'm tellin yeh all this stuff about RTE an I'm inclined to forget yeh might know shag-all about Cork or Ireland. Call here to me when I do that.

"Don't tell us tis Gay Byrne!" said Liam.

Right: Gay Byrne – presentur of our big talk show, the

Late Late.

"God, Liam, Gay's the *only* straight man on RTE," said Dec. "To think of it! The cultural life of the nation in the hands of a bunch a Dublin faggots! I'm surprised at you, Missy Scarlett – I thought you'd have the good taste to go for a southernur and a gentleman."

"He's a Corkman."

"Come out now!" said Liam, steppin back. "So what's his name?"

"Kevin."

"Oh, that RTE fella from Kilcrea Park?" said Liam.

Dec looked at him pityingly. "Kilcrea Park? Are yeh joking? That *boring* middle-class *purgatory* couldn't produce a gay man if it bent over backwards – if it bent *double*! Get real!" Dec has an awful thing about Kilcrea Park because that's where Liz's boyfriend comes from an he's jealous. As a matter a fact Kilcrea Park, for a small little place, has produced more than its fair share a quare-hawks – weird types I mean, not faggots like.

"His name's Kevin Fitzpatrick," said poor Tizzy who nevur evur knew when those two chansurs were razzin him. "An he comes from Blackrock."

"Oh, very very classy!" said Liam.

"No wondur we nevur heard of him," said Dec.

At this point we were interrupted by a bunch a laney boys outside the Sportsbowl across the street shoutin at us. "*Steamurs! Steamurs!*"

"Jesus!" said Dec, throwin the chin up.

"C'man an we move," said Tizzy, blushin.

"Listen," said Liam, throwin the gang across the road a dirty look. "Will we do Pana? Or go down to Slick's?"

"*Steamurs!* Come ovur an give us a gobble-job!"

"Jesus!" said Dec again. "I mean, in broad daylight! But c'mere – aren't we were takin Tony up to the Good Shepherds?"

A moment's panic came ovur me like a hand clutchin me heart. I didn't know why. The Good Shepherds was what I wanted, wasn't it?

"Tony?" asked Tizzy an the voice shook an the face went pale.

"We've got his ashes here." Liam made to take the urun outa the bag.

"Not in fronta the Garda Station, yeh eejit," said Dec, stoppin his hand. They started movin along MacCurtain Street an Liam told Tizzy about what Dec called my demise an my last wishes. Poor Tizzy was in tears, flickin em away with his fingurs. Very soft, Tizzy is.

We passed Slick's an went off down past St Maries a the Isle an up Sunday's Well. Twas one a those bright days when Cork manages to look good – the way it climbs all the hills around the city. An me sayin to meself why did I evur leave it.

But Dec was back on the Big Dick story. "As soon as the door closed he was on top of me. *Rampant!* I was so pissed off I used the oldest excuse in the book: I'm sorry, I've got a headache. Anyway: I woke up in the middle of the night. I didn't know what woke me first. And then I saw yer man. He was dancing. In front of the mirror. With this *monstrosity* between his legs bouncing up and down. *Dancing. Nude.*" He hadta stop an wait for the lads to get ovur that one. Laugh! They were drinkin their tears.

"That was it. I'd had it. I mean, imagine, for the rest of your born days, nevur knowing when you'd wake up to a sight like that! C'man, will ye?"

We'd arrived at the drive up to the Good Shepherds. Me heart was in me mouth. You could feel the peace while we were climbin up to the convent. But why had I this flutterin in the pit a me stomach? The buildin is long an red-brick with towurs an things – not to be confused with the Mad House that we call The Red Brick furthur out the

27

rivur a bit. There are huge trees. There was this kinda prayurful silence.

"What are we goin to do?" asked Liam. "Are we goin to ask permission or what?"

"Hould yer horses," said Dec. "This is a recce."

"An what's that while we're at it?" asks Liam.

"God! Look! I've only been to *one* war picture in my life and that was *Kelly's Heroes* that my mothur took me to after my Confirmation – I've nevur forgiven hur – why she thought I'd like that butch crap I don't know – but even I know what a recce is!"

"Oh, yeh mean like a recon*nay*sance?" Liam.

"Oh, pardon me if I didn't get the correct term – that's what comes a leaving school at fourteen." Which he did. But a course he's always mad readin an yeh'd nevur guess it – that he hadn't his Leavin I mean. He was a bit huffy at times about it because Liam does have his Leavin. I do meself.

There were a few nuns floatin around an a few Magdalens (Fallen Women like). It used to be a thrivin orphanage an penitentiary (Dec's word) for Fallen Women in the old days an all the childrun a Cork used to be threatened with bein sent up to the Good Shepherds. Nowadays all the young wans are walkin around town with buggies – eithur that or hoppin ovur to England for long weekends. There's a slump in the Orphan Industry.

Myself, I call that progress.

The graveyard is beyond the convent an highur up – a small little place in the far cornur with a wall an railin around it.

When we got there we stood lookin at the grave.

"They're onta us," said Liam, pointin. Undur the statue a the Infant a Prague with his ball an crown an the gravestone, there was a metal sign sayin: Reconnaissance à la Petite Nellie. France 1934.

"God, what's it like to be thick ignorant?" said Dec. "That means 'in memory of'."

"*He's got the whole woruld in his hand,*" sang Liam softly at the Infant with his ball. "*He's got the whole woruld in his hand, he's got . . .* "

They knelt down an pretended to be prayin.

"Talking of balls, Tizzy," muttured Dec after a while. "Does Bosco know he's only gettin half a bargain in you?"

"I told him. Yeah."

"Straight up – that's our Tizzy," muttured Dec.

"*How great is the Holy One,*" sang Liam. "How does it go, Dec? *That lau-aunched his flo-oating balls, that lau-aunched his floating balls . . .* "

"Liam," Dec hissed undur his breath. "There's a nun keeping an eye on us. Shut up!"

They shut up. Sure enough there was an ould nun dodderin around among the graves an she lookin daggurs at em.

"D'ye see the problem?" muttured Dec aftur a while.

"Yeah," said Liam.

"What is it?" Tizzy whispured.

"The mosaic," said Dec.

"What about it?"

"We can't scattur Tony over that! They'd just come an sweep him up."

"He should've thought a that," said me brothur. Bitch!

"Last wishes are last wishes," said Dec, very severe.

The nun shuffled off back to the convent. We got up to have a look around.

That graveyard always fascinated me. Twas Dec brought me there the first time. An told me all about Little Nellie, how she was raised by the nuns an how she died a consumption when she was only four an how a statue a the Infant a Prague used to dance for hur. I didn't believe any a that but twas kinda nice hearin Dec tellin about it.

The othur gravestones were amazin too. Sister Francis Xavier O'Brien, Sister Thérèse of the Infant of Prague O'Hanrahan, Mother Mary of Perpetual Succour McCarthy. Some a the dates went back to 1841 an thereabouts. The lads wandured around havin a laugh at the names an Dec started talkin about his early memories of his Aunty Aggie takin him up to the Good Shepherds to see Little Nellie's grave.

"I rembur that day because I realised what I wanted to be when I grew up – one of the nuns I saw moving around between the graves. They looked so beautiful! I knew that was what I wanted to be. It didn't occur to me at that time that it was impossible."

"You musta felt you were a girl, so," said Liam.

"I dunno. I always knew there was something different about me. I mean I was born the way I am. It's not a 'sickeness', as they say. I knew, I knew from a very early age. I couldn't put a name on it. But when I was seven this cousin of mine came down from Dublin. He was in the army and the first time I saw him I was turned on like. I mean I was seven years of age and I was turned on. I was to share my bed with him but I wouldn't. You know – God! I've *regretted* it since – to this *day*!"

Next thing he started expoundin all he knew about the Good Shepherds. An he knew everythin because he'd done a spell there when he was fifteen, workin in the laundry dressed up as a girl. I'll tell yeh more about that latur. Founded in France aftur the Revolution, he said, for rescuin Fallen Women. Then he started on about othur ordurs. "Do ye know that the Trappists are buried in open coffins? Then they pull out the bottom board an the corpse flops into the grave. Y'see, the idea is, tis a communal coffin."

They didn't know. They didn't believe it eithur. They said so. "That's a fuckin lie. Tis disgustin anyway. Sick!"

"It's not! I think it's *beautiful*!" With his voice crackin on the 'beautiful' an a kinda little shake a the body to make it strongur. "Like when Thomas Merton talks about the grim smile of satisfaction Trappist corpses wear."

A grim smile a satisfaction? Like Leonard Cohen?

"Hey, Dec, should we just leave the urun on the grave?" Liam asked, very uncertain.

"Out of the question. Didn't they have the grave covured with ex votos before until they removed them 'for reasons of prudence', whatevur that means."

"X *what*?"

"Ex votos – offerings from people fulfilling a vow – like people who've been cured an come an leave things in thanksgiving – like crutches an surgical boots an glassy-eyes . . . the odd kidney or two . . . "

"I thought they were some kinda condom," said Liam.

"Alas, no . . . wouldn't it be an ideal world if poor Tony could have come here an hung up his condom."

They said nothin for a while.

Tizzy spoke up at last. "But why did he want to be scattured here anyway? Maybe twas de only place he could tink of at de time?"

Dec nearly exploded. "Right! So twould be alright if we just scattured him up the Lough to feed the swans?"

"On the *south* side?" said Liam. "Jaysis, at least we'd bring him ovur to the North Gate Bridge an feed our own swans! Like the two Glin supporturs in the joke!" The Glen is the North Side hurlin team in case yeh don't know.

"Look. He wanted to be scattured and I'm goin to scattur him if tis the last thing I do! Come on. We'll have to think about this." An he started off down the drive.

I was so elated I could've flown. I shoulda been able to. Wasn't I a spirit? Shouldn't I be inta waftin around an all that? An here I was, strangled in the stink a Liam's dirty socks. Oh, for the wings, for the wings of a dove . . . But I didn't care. I was still where I wanted to be. With the lads. With *Dec*.

When that thought came to me I seemed to go *whoosh* an I imagined meself soarin in spirit down that drive. Could a spirit have an out-a-the-body experience? I tried. I imagined meself soarin over Dec's left shouldur – like his Guardian Anjul. The mental effort was too much though – a couple a minutes high an *wham*! Back I slammed into the dirty socks. So much for mind ovur mattur.

Down across the Shaky Bridge with us an along through Fitzgerald's Park. They hadta stop then at the Tea House an have tea because Dec fancies the guy there – a tall thin blonde type – straight unfortunately. ("God, I could bonk him senseless – gutless!") They sat inside, surrounded by all the university people, where they could be lampin him. I was delighted with life, just listenin to the crap they d'be goin on with an lookin at Dec's eyes glintin in the sunshine through the winda.

Twas a moment a great content for me. Jesus, if I coulda been half as content when I was in the flesh like! I started thinkin a how different I'd be if I'd a chance to live me life again. For starturs, if I had all me equipment again, if I was sittin there with them in the flesh, the first thing I'd do would be to lean across an give Dec the sweetest kiss he evur got in his born days. An as for all the people in the Tea House an what they might think, well shag em an the whole a Cork for that mattur an the whole fuckin world that would nevur let me be myself. Let em all go fuck themselves an let me take care a me own heart's desire.

An maybe I'd kiss Tizzy too for good measure. Jesus, the mouth on that boy!

Anyway, there I was rantin at the world when I was the one who'd fucked up an found meself dead like a right eejit. As for kissin Dec an Tizzy, I coulda done that any day a me life if I'd put me mind to it. But I'd nevur realised twas worth doin. Actually, to be honest with yeh, like a lot a fellas I always had a kinda problem about kissin. Like twas too – I dunno – too *exposin*? But what the fuck, now.

I felt like a different person by the time we left the Tea House. Twas a bit late like, I know. I mean I was *dead*. Bettur late than nevur? Anyway, I felt ready to stand up an be counted. Like: so you think I'm peculiar? I'm a spirit in an urun. And you're not. Well, fuck *you*! This is what I am.

Inta town with us an me on a high.

We parted from Tizzy in St Augustine Street – it's just a lane actually. Dec wanted to have a look at the bookshop in The Othur Place. Then they'd have a cuppa in the café so they could be readin the dykes for the way they d'be climbin all ovur each othur an sayin how disgustin an ovur the top they are. I knew it all of old.

"Are yeh goin to de club to*niiiight*?" Tizzy called back when he was halfway down the lane.

"I *am*, are *yooouuu*?" screeched Liam in his best Cork singsong, hittin the sky with his "yoouuuuu."

Twas an old joke. I still thought twas funny, dead an all as I was.

"*I'll* be dere if *you*'ll be dere will *you* be dere dough?" Tizzy sang back, his voice see-sawin.

"And people tryin to pray inside St Augustine's," said Dec. "You'd be mortified!"

CHAPTER 2

IT GAVE ME A QUEER FEELIN GOIN INTA THE CLUB THAT NIGHT. Like I'd a lump in me throat. Especially when I saw Mothur ensconced in his usual position, cigarette ensconced in its usual position. Our club is a great place – a bit makeshift as far as furniture goes, with wooden benches like, but tis all decked out with scenury an bits a lightin an stuff robbed from the Everyman an othur theatres an places round the city.

Mothur's an artist an does well for himself – no shortage a dosh but he spends a ferocious amount. His real name is Denis, by the way, Denis Harte. Yeh mighta heard a him or seen him on RTE or seen his pictures. Lean-lookin man – piercin blue eyes. Nice-lookin. At *least* ten years oldur than us – maybe more like fifteen. Bit of a beard, or a berd as the ould folk would say, just very little, y'know the kinda thing – brownyfair.

Anyway, as I was sayin, most a the scenury was swiped an half of it from RTE an the Eurovision Song Contest years ago an brought down from Dublin in the back of a van.

When we went in they were all dancin *mad* as usual.

The clones an chickuns were there in full force an the place was full a women too – the dykes an the hoors an the fag-hags an the odd woman chancin her arm with a man. A lot a the lads bring their sisturs with em – y'see this is a kinda traditional thing to do by way of havin a woman to parade yerself with. We had ta shouldur our way through em all to get to Mothur's table. The noise wasn't exactly disco-level because we don't have the equipment like but twas deafenin enough. He looked up at us through the usual cloud a smoke, a bevy a rings on his fingurs an a bevy a pints before him. Plus a bottle a Paddy, three-quarters full. The pints would be ones he'd bought for othur people – he only drank whiskey an vodka an white an gins an tonics an the like himself. Jay, twas great to see him. He was flanked (that's a grand word for it) by Mad Mary an one a his favourite chickuns who looked right sulky to see us. The chickuns, in case yeh don't know, are a whole troop a lads who keep appearin out a nowhere (an endless supply, Mothur says) newly gay, newly decked out in their gay attire, all around seventeen an eighteen. They're very wild, at least some of em are.

"Benedicite," said Dec. Chapter 63, that is. *Whenever the brethren meet, let the junior ask the senior for a blessing*.

"Daaaahlings! How are you! Liam! How good to see you!" An they both got kissed. "Declan, come sit here next to me and hold my hand. I'm *most* depressed, *hideously* depressed!"

Dec glared at Mad Mary, who was in drag as usual that night, till he made room for him next to Mothur.

"Where's your boa?" said Dec, lookin down his nose at Mad Mary's legs. "Shouldn't you be out on the floor flaunting yourself?"

"Fuck aafff, baaoy!" I'm guessin now but I'd say Mad Mary didn't know what boa or flauntin meant.

"Pardon me now, Mr Harte, but your catamite is giving me terrible abuse. Don't you evur correct him? If I were you I'd take him home and *ledder* him for his own good. It's this liberal upbringing that has the youth of this country ruined . . . "

35

"Oh, please, please, *please*, I *beg* of you, don't start squabbling – I couldn't stand it tonight! Liam – but you're looking absolutely marvellous, my dear! And how is the Great Metropolis? Seething in Sin as usual, I trust? Excellent, excellent," He distributed pints a Murphy's from the fleetful in fronta him. "Declan, *what* are you *doing* to me? My flat is in a *disgusting* state – like the proverbial rubbish-tip. It's no wonder I'm depressed. Now it's *your* fault, dear boy – you know it is. *Why* haven't you been by? You *know* I depend on you!" Dec has been cleanin Mothur's flat for years.

"Didn't they tell you I was away?" asked Dec, a bit aggressive like.

"They may have, they may have . . . perhaps they did . . . it may be I didn't absorb the information . . . " Mothur was a *ferocious* drinker. "But where *were* you, daahling?"

"Swansea."

"*Swan*sea?"

"On my way to London. But I turned back."

"London! But you mustn't *dream* of leaving Cork! I cannot survive without you – I would *recidivate*!"

Recidivate. That's what he said, I'm sure of it. I don't know what it means. But I can guess. He meant that him an his flat would go to the dogs.

"You're right there, girl," said Liam. "That flat was shaggin awful before Regina started workin for yeh – a total wreck like."

"He changed my life! Will I ever forget it? That happy day! Here's my list before I start, said he to me, handing me this *lengthy* document – a veritable *catalogue* of cleaning equipment. Ah, blessed words if I did but know it at the time!" Mothur seemed a bit distracted. He kept lookin at the door an the fact that he was talkin so much an wavin his hands about meant he was nervous.

"Yeah, an then he went out an spent the money on

drink an he had to wait for dole-day to buy the cleanin stuff!"

"But he *did* buy it," said Mothur. "And came – "

"With my little magic wand," said Dec.

"Oh, he's a wonder . . . " said Mothur.

Tis true. I've seen him at it. Like he'd go in an he'd be *scrubbin mad*, gettin the whole place spick an span an throwin things out. An then he'd say "If you're lookin for anything now tis out in the bin" an that kinda thing. An then when he'd be finished Mothur would produce a bottle a whiskey an they'd sit down an they'd polish it off between em. He's done it for a few people besides Mothur too.

"And how he pampers me!" said Mothur. "Cooking and running after me with cups of coffee, making me sit down, telling me 'not to budge now'. I need it, I need it, my *soul* needs it."

"But doesn't Mad Mary do all that for yeh?" asked Liam slyly.

"Fuck aafff!" said Mad Mary.

"Mary has his own function, dahling, and it has little to do with the kitchen." Mad Mary smirked at this, twirlin his long black hair – well, his hair-piece like – around his fingurs.

"That's *his* mistake. There's more powur in the kitchen," said Dec. "That's why wherevur I was I'd wangle my way into the kitchen by hook or by crook. And anothur thing," eyein Mad Mary. "I wouldn't be seen *dead* in a mini-skirt if I had knobbly knees like that. Which I haven't, thanks be to God."

"Declan! Please! I really cannot *stand* bitchiness tonight. Listen to me – tell me, must chaos come again? Have you deserted me?"

"Will you stop *moaning*? I'll be down tomorrow. A dab of Pledge behind the ears and I'll sort you out in no time.

Shur, I have your place now to a fine art."

"Thank you, thank you, thank you!" An he filled a glass up to the top with whiskey for Dec. He was gazin at the door again. I saw Liam takin that in an smilin inta his pint. "Really! Liam, dear, could you go and ask them to put on some decent music? One can only take so much of that dance stuff. Ask them to play Annie Lennox perhaps."

"Why not some Joan Suthurland?" said Dec. "Tell them there's a request for the quartet from *Rigoletto*."

No soonur did he say that but the speakurs began to blare out Hammur's *U Can't Touch This* an twas like a signal for everybody to clear the floor. All the clones an chickuns lined up for this kind of dance-competition they do. The clones were all decked out in rap gear. The original clones were back a bit, in the late 70s maybe – they'd all dress the same, very sharp, in suits, an if they were a bit butch they'd have a moustache. They useta fox-trot with each othur all night an do this kinda jivin off each othur. An now we call the Hammur crowd "clones" because they all dress the same too.

"Oh, Good Lord, No! It's Spanner-time!" Mothur was definitely cranky tonight. He usually liked watchin the chickuns in action.

Music hits me so hard, rapped Hammur with the chickuns an clones backin him.

Makes me say oh my Lord!

"Don't ye want to dance?" said Dec to Mad Mary an the chickun, real aggressive. He didn't like Mary an he didn't approve a the chickuns at all. He was always givin out about them bein too young, sayin twas immoral altogethur – which was queer because he was on the game himself since he was fourteen – on the game, not just on the scene like. Although he always said he nevur took money – that he done it because he *liked* doin it. Maybe. Anyway, like me, in the early days he'da been scared a his mothur.

I told you Home Boy! shouted Hammur.

U can't touch dis! screamed the chickuns an the clones.

"Well? Aren't yeh going to dance?" said Dec to Mary in his spit-in-yer-eye tone that went with crossed legs an a straight back an the chin up.

"I mise well," said Mad Mary an he an the chickun got up.

"Be careful now! Don't fall on anyone off those heels or we'll have the Gardaí ovur!" called Dec aftur him, real bitchy. "If he fell on yeh, he'd kill yeh with a nose like that!" Mad Mary had a kinda hatchet-face with a real sharp nose. "An would yeh look at those legs? Wouldn't he covur em up? I dunno, Denis, I don't know how yeh can look at that poxy-lookin face in the bed next to yeh. An just for the sake of havin a body there! Jesus, I dunno – whatevur I done I nevur done that! I mean I have my pride. I'd want to be attracted to em anyway."

Hammur was goin strong.

Yo I told you

U can't touch this . . .

Mothur was makin a face as if he had a toothache. He let out a shudderin sigh an threw back anothur whiskey.

"Daaahlings, I'm so *hideously* depressed!"

"Will yeh stop *moaning*?" said Dec. "Who wants to listen to that kind of misury? Can't you offer it up for the Souls in Purgatory? How about a few aspirations? All for Thee, O Heart of Jesus, all for Thee? Do you say your morning offering? I offer Thee all the prayurs, works and *suffurings* of this day . . . I mean to say, what I want to know is: where is Our Lady in your life?"

You talkin bout a show

That's hot and tight –

Mothur waved a hand as if he was tryin to wave Hammur away. "Declan, you're forgetting I'm a Protestant. We don't go in for Mariolatry – "

"That's what leaves ye as ye are! Think of Mary, Queen of Scots so . . . "

"Why on earth, dear boy, should I think of Mary Queen of Scots?" But he sounded real intrigued.

Dec was goin to tell him anyway, intrigued or not. "Well, think of her imprisoned in Tutbury Castle in the damp draughty rooms above the privies and the stench in her nostrils day and night . . . "

Legit
Either work hard
Or you might as well quit . . .

The clones were at their best, struttin their stuff. The wildness of the chickuns couldn't touch that.

"I mean, think of her courage! I bet she wasn't *moaning* the way you are . . . "

"Whasupitcha anyway, girl?" Liam asked Mothur.

"Oh, nothing new, nothing new . . . " said Mothur with a sigh.

"Oh," said Liam winkin at Dec. "Tis the lash with the gash, is it? Still nothin doin?"

Stop! Hammur-time!

Mothur was starin at Liam as if he was goin to claim him. "To *whom* are you referring in that *disgusting* manner?"

"Sorry," said Liam. "Joke. I meant: is it only Mike?"

"*Only* Mike? *Only* Mike? The grandest, purest passion in my life and you say is it *only* Mike?" Mothur ground out his cigarette furiously. "Have you no souls? You're dross! Dross!"

"Take it *easy*," said Dec. "There's no call for foul language. And listen, if it's Mike is the cause of all this *misury* can I offur you a word of advice?"

Mothur nodded, makin an effort to control himself.

"Next time he's down at your place why don't you just take him into the bedroom an fuck him an be done with it?"

Mothur's eyes were startin from his head. If he had a knife in his hand he'd have gutted him. He didn't answur for ages.

"Well?" asked Dec finally.

Mothur was makin furthur efforts to calm himself – deep breathin an all that. "Wasn't it you who warned me to move cautiously and watch my step?"

"That was two years ago," answured Dec. "The suspense is killing me. I can only imagine what it's doing to you."

"Talk a the devil," said Liam an he cocked an eyebrow at the dance-floor. "Will yeh look at the gaatch a that!"

Mike had come in an was break-dancin with the clones. He had it all: the hat an the kinky hair an the belts an the jacket an the make-up. The only way he looked different from Michael Jackson, as far as yeh could see, is that he had a bunch a earrings in one ear an he doesn't have the Peter Pan nose – yet. He doesn't have the Cork beak eithur – no, a fine straight nose he has an Mothur gets the horrors dreamin that he's had a job done on it.

Mike is different anyway – yeh wouldn't need any crystal ball to tell that his mothur musta been a brassur who'd spent many a long night traipsin the docks. He has a fair oul touch a the tar-brush – he'd get away with the dark eyes an the black hair but not the olive skin, here in Cork where even the blackest a the Black Irish look like Snow White. But now the question was ac . . . wha d'yeh say? When yeh mean it doesn't matter a fuck anyway? Aca-something. Oh yeah, academic. Anyway, what I'm tryin to say is that he was so plastured with make-up that yeh couldn't hope to see what colour he was any more.

"Aaaaah!" That was Mothur.

Yeh see, the thing is, Mothur had a real thing for Mike for ages, even before he became Michael Jackson, because Mike (if he evur had anothur name I've long forgotten it)

useta sing all these romantic bluesy kinda songs an Mothur
would be "Oh God! Isn't he wonderful? Listen to him, isn't
he marvellous! He's beautiful!" an all that. But what
happened was that before he'd a chance to get anywhere
Mike became MJ an took a vow a celibacy because he read
that MJ doesn't have a sex life an this was the bane a
Mothur's life an he used to read the newspapurs every day
in the hopes that there'd be a big sex scandal involvin
Michael Jackson. He useta make em up like doodlin –
there'd be scraps a papur lyin around him with things like
Michael Jackson absconds with chauffeur written on em –
or *Michael entertains Chippendales at Neverland*. He
figured this was his only hope with our Mike. An in the
meantime Mad Mary was doin the job Mike wouldn't take
on for love or money.

"Jaysis, here's Tizzy!" said Liam. "What's happened to
yur man? To Bosco? Why's he so early? Jaysis, I hope he
isn't aftur gettin beaten again!" Tizzy was always gettin
beaten. He'd go down the quays – I mean he's a divil for
goin down there – an he gets beaten – the queer-bashin
thing. He's been beaten so many times, Tizzy has, he's
always bein jumped an beaten an people sayin don't be
goin on yur own any more. He could be beaten by some
fella who'd pick him up, take him round the cornur an give
him a ledderin. Or hopped by gangs. There's an awful
violent scene but we ostracise anyone who's inta that.
Anyway, poor Tizzy with his one ball is like a magnet to
those types an he gets beaten all the time. Course we can
nevur figure out whethur he likes it – those situations.

"No, he's alright," said Dec as Tizzy made for us
because Tizzy was grinnin all ovur his face.

"Where's Bosco, boy?' Liam called at him.

Tizzy stood at our table, clappin his hands togethur, all
flushed in the face. "I lost me cherries! I lost me cherries!"

"G'waan!" said Liam, amazed. "D'yeh mean with

Bosco?" We nevur thought Tizzy'd do it – I mean he'd been down the quays for years an around the Golden Triangle (that's the trawlin-ground between Connolly Hall an the Cats and Dogs an the docks – yeh can flake off there yurself if yeh ever feel so horny yeh'd get up on a gust) an he'd nevur done it in all that time.

"Oh, tell the whole world, do!" said Dec.

"No, I did, I lost me cherries!" Tizzy was delighted with himself.

"If you run down, *The Irish Times* office might still be open next door – you could put it in the late edition," said Dec, pointin with the full stretch a his arm. "Go on! Run! *Go dtí an oifig! Rith!*"

Tizzy sat down, all excited. "Why didn't ye tell me? Why didn't ye tell me? Tis only like goin to de toilet!"

"My God," groaned Mothur, coverin his eyes with his hand an shakin his head. "There are times . . . "

Liam was in hysterics. Dec just sat there lookin outraged but I could tell he was lovin it.

"Dat's what it felt like to me anyway," said Tizzy.

"Tell us more!" said Dec like a schoolmistress. "Give us the details like! Don't be coy now whatevur you do!"

"But was it Bosco?" asked Liam.

"Yeah!"

"So where is he now?"

"He's aftur goin back."

"To Dublin?"

"Yeah . . . "

"Already? Jay, he mustn't have been much impressed by your performance," said Liam.

"Why didn't you fake it?" asked Dec.

Tizzy looked hurt. "No, yeh see he didn't bring his car so he had to catch de half-nine train . . . "

"Wait a minute now," Dec cut in. "Let me get this straight. *When* did this great event take place? I thought you weren't meeting him till half-eight?"

"Yeah. We had a drink in de bar – in de Met – an den we went up to his room."

"And?"

"He said we'd ten minutes before de train . . . "

Everyone started laughin except Dec.

"Are yeh *serious* like?" said Dec.

"Yeah . . . "

"*Ten minutes before the train!* Are yeh *serious?*" Dec was scandalised. "I don't believe this!"

"He was lovely . . . " sighed Tizzy. "He said he was tinkin a me all day . . . "

"*Ten minutes before the train!* God, some people would do anything for the couple a bob!"

"What d'yeh mean? Twas grand . . . he was lovely . . . "

"Have yeh no pride? God, these Dublin faggots down here corrupting the youth!" With a toss a the head.

"How much did yeh make?" Always practical, me brothur Liam.

"Thiry quid."

"Yeh *eejit!*" said Liam. "Yeh stupid langur! Holy Jesus, but you've no business sense! D'yeh realise how much yeh couldn've made? For *that*? An you a virgin an all?" Now Liam was outraged – at the waste a Tizzy's assets.

"For five minutes being savaged?" said Dec. "I don't think he did badly at all!"

"Savaged? I wasn't savaged!" Poor Tizzy was upset. "He was lovely, I tell yeh! He was real gentle . . . "

"Of course he was. *Certainly* he was. He must have given a full minute – sixty full seconds – to foreplay. That's a real gentleman, no doubt about it. Or did he just say 'Bend ovur'? Is he married, by the way? Sounds the type." Dec was really actin the maggot. He could be a right bitch at times. He could say really hurtful things an the more he drank the worse he got.

"Tizzy," said Mothur in a voice that made me remembur how much I liked him. "If the experience was – ah, as you described it . . . "

"Only like goin to the toilet," put in Liam.

"Thank you, Liam," said Mothur, wincin an puttin his hand to his forehead. Then he took Tizzy's hand an patted it. "If the experience was – ah, like that, he certainly was gentle. I'm sure he *was* as you say 'lovely' – you must have felt really – ah, relaxed with him. So never mind Declan. He's just jealous because he can't do it . . . " The last bit was plain divilment to get a rise outa Dec.

"*Excuse* me, now," said Dec. "I can do it if I want to. But why anyone *wants* to do it is beyond me. There was this married woman I was talking to once. Tis just a mattur of relaxing, says she to me. A married woman! I think that's scandalous!"

Mothur laughed outright at this. "Remind me to lend you my Derek Jarman tomorrow. His notion is that every man needs to be fucked – that it gives one an outlook on life that cannot be acquired in any other way . . . "

"*No, thank you,*" said Dec. "I'll stick with *I Leaped ovur the Wall* . . . "

"Easy now," said Mothur suddenly undur his breath. Mike an Mad Mary were comin up to the table togethur.

Mike sat down next to Liam. Mothur looked like he had a toothache again. Mad Mary sat next to Mothur an clung hurself up agin him. Mike sat there starin at his hands.

"How are you, sweetheart?" Mothur asked Mike.

"Fine," said Mike without raisin his eyes or his voice or anythin else. So the fact that Mad Mary was tryin to grope Mothur had no effect on him.

"*Heal the World*'s doin really well in the charts," said Liam, real chatty. "Still in the European Top Ten since before Christmas. Great goin. What's your next release goin to be? Oh, *Give in to me*, isn't it?"

No response at all from Mike. He sat there like a martyr. He's good at that.

"How much has *Dangerous* sold now? Twenty million copies, isn't it? An then they say yeh're losin yur grip – bullshit."

Nothin from Mike.

"Oh, I get it," said Liam. "No interviews. I saw your attorney on MTV givin a press conference the othur day. By the way, *The National Enquirur* says you're a deaf mute an your songs are all lipsynced. What d'yeh have to say to that?"

Mike coulda been sittin all by himself on the Polar icecap watchin penguins for all the reaction he gave to all a this.

"Jay, but he's lucky he don't think he's Eddie Murphy," said Liam. "Imagine havin to crack jokes all the time an talk jive an all that – 'haul ass' an 'covur your ass' an 'kick ass' an 'kiss ass' – "

"An not to get them mixed up," said Dec.

"Twould be completely beyond yeh," said Liam to Mike, shakin his head.

"Liam, you're completely out-of-date," said Mothur, all anxious to defend Mike. "Didn't you see the Oprah Winfrey interview? Michael Jackson is actually quite an articulate person . . . "

"Shur, that was a total fraud, didn't yeh hear?" says Liam. "Y'see it turns out that Oprah is a ventriloquist."

They had a great laugh at that one. Even Mike smiled.

"But I don't understand yeer interest in those people," said Dec. "Forgive me for saying it, Mike, but that Michael Jackson really pisses me off. I was reading the othur day that Eddie Murphy or somebody went to lunch with him and d'yeh know what they had to eat? *Peanutbutter* sandwiches. *Peanutbutter* sandwiches. All that money and they have *peanutbutter* sandwiches. I mean I've no time for that sort of thing!" He really meant it – his eyes were opened wide an sparkin in a way I know. "That's nothing but affectation!"

This rang a bell with Mothur. "Socrates, I think, was walking in the market-place," says he, wavin his fag. "Oh dear . . . was it Socrates?"

"Don't worry," said Dec. "Socrates won't sue – not this week anyway."

"Socrates was walking in the market-place," said Mothur. "And he saw some richly attired Epicureans. Look, said he," pointin the cigarette. "Affectation! Then a little while later he saw some Stoics . . . or was it Spartans? Oh dear . . . "

"Denis," said Liam. "We don't give a shit. Will yeh go on an tell us the story?"

"He saw some . . . eh, Stoics. Very simply dressed with no decoration whatsoever. Look, said he," an the cigarette went out again. "More affectation!"

"Isn't that what I just said?" said Dec. "My very words! Socrates, no less!"

"Not that I think Michael Jackson is affected," said Mothur quickly, suddenly realisin where his story had led him. His eyes opened wide in his alarm. "On the contary, I think he's extremely genuine! *Extremely* genuine! I was *most impressed* by that interview." Lookin anxiously at Mike who had his dark eyes fastened on Mothur's face as if he was one a the movin statues from Ballywhatsitsname. "No doubt he *likes* peanutbutter sandwiches." Lookin even more frantic. "I do myself!"

Everybody was starin at Mothur now. In amazement – wonderin what he was goin to come out with next.

"Pathetic," said Dec.

Mothur copped himself on at last. He threw back his whiskey. "Michael Jackson," he muttered inta his glass. "My nem-" Well, he said his nem-somethin-or-othur but I didn't catch it.

"Your what?" Liam wanted to know.

"Oh, nothing, nothing," muttured Mothur.

"By the way, don't anyone think now that Mad Mary has her hand in Mothur's crotch," said Dec. "I have a good vantage point – like 'view' to you – here and I can assure you all that her hand is a half-inch – no, let me be fair now, a *full inch* away from his crotch. So don't get the wrong idea whatevur ye do."

"Fuck aafff, baaoy!" said Mad Mary. "Mind yur own fuckin business!"

"That's the only thing that appeals to me about you, Mary – your eloquence," said Dec.

Mothur waved a hand in an irritated way but then he put Mad Mary's two hands up on the table as if to end the argument.

Mike looked up. "How's Tony?" he asked. I could've kissed him. I could see Mothur do a little double-take when he realised he was aftur forgettin to ask.

"He's gone," said Liam. "That's why I'm home." He dipped into the bag an pulled me out an set me on the table. They all stared an no-one said anythin.

Hey sister, go sister, soul sister, go sister –

Labelle was startin up with *Lady Marmalade*.

"How was it at the end?" asked Mothur, rubbin the cornur of his eye with the cigarette hand.

I was listenin to the music.

Struttin her stuff on the street

She said: Hello, Joe, you wanna give it a go?

Everyone was struttin like mad on the floor.

"Oh, not too bad," answered Liam. "Not as bad as I'd expected. They had him doped up to the eyeballs. He didn't know anyone. He didn't know me." He was silent awhile an then he went on. "I'm sorry he didn't – know me, I mean. I nevur got a chance to say goodbye or anythin."

"You're very brave, my dear," said Mothur softly an the hand with the fag poised rubbed the back a Liam's hand.

The hand-movements were brilliant on the floor. Yeh could see they all imagined themselves dressed up in feathurs an silvur bikinis. Great costumes, that video.

Me brothur blinked hard an I thought he was goin to cry again. He'd done a lot a cryin in London. The night before we left he'd cried himself to sleep clutchin me to his face so the urun got all wet with tears. Twas terrible because I could do nothin to comfort him. I didn't want that to happen again.

Dec, I said, do somethin . . .

"We're going to have a big farewell for him up at the Good Shepherds," said Dec. "That's what he wanted and to have his ashes scattured up there. The nuns are going to lay on tea and there will be a guest list – select, of course." With a look at Mad Mary. He stated all this as a straight fact – he wasn't campin it up or anythin.

Liam stared at him like he was ravin mad an his mouth dropped open.

"Oh, lovely," said Mothur. "Did you arrange all that?"

"Oh, I'm well in up there," said Dec.

Mothur believed him. Why wouldn't he? We all knew about Dec an the nuns. "When will it be?"

"We haven't decided yet."

Fuckin right we hadn't.

Just then Liz arrived. "Will yeh look at yer man," was her greetin, pointin at Dec. "London, how are yeh!" Dec started smirkin an tossed his head – delighted to see hur. Then she spotted Liam. "Liam!" says she an threw hur arms around him. An then twas all about how Sistur Breeda who runs the home for the retarded kids was askin for him an the ould codgers in the Simon House were missin him an all that. Liam was dead pleased, I could see, though he didn't let on. He's mad for that kinda work. Dec, too.

Like I said, Liz wasn't gay. Dec an Liam met hur doin that mentally-handicapped stuff an then she came knockin at the door a the club one day: "Would ye like a hand?" I suppose she thought we were handicapped too. Disadvantaged Persons. So Dec an hurself became great pals. Yeh'd take hur to be a dyke really – no make-up like an the jeans an the flat shoes. She nevur dressed up fancy like the fag-hags did – but she wasn't butch eithur. Pretty, small, blondy, wavy springy hair, very fair-skinned an rosy-cheeked. Roundish bright face, bright blue eyes. Always laughin. Yeah, that's Liz. Middle-class. College student.

Right: *Ring My Bell.* Would that yeh could like.

They all got up to dance. Yeh see, we have a whole pile a these ancient records from the 70s that tis a kinda tradition to dance to. They all moved off an this left Mothur an Mike facin each othur ovur me on the table.

You can ring my be-e-ell!

You can ring my bell

Ting-a-ling-a-ling . . .

I wished I could get up an dance. It seemed the kinda thing a spirit should do. I mean anjuls dance, don't they? At Christmas. On top a stables? And Eastur? On top a tombs an things? But I wasn't an anjul. Maybe that was the snag. While I was thinkin this, Mothur put a long fingur on the urun an stroked it in a circle. Twas funny the way people wanted to touch me.

"Ash Wednesday," said Mothur. "Remember man thou art but dust and into dust thou shalt return. Tony's just gone a bit faster than the rest of us . . . " I don't know if he was comfortin himself or Mike. Mike was lookin at him wide-eyed. He looked miserable.

Wooooooooooo Wooooooo went everyone on the dance-floor.

"Remember meeting me on Ash Wednesday?" Mothur went on. "I met you by chance on Patrick Street early and took you into Bewley's for breakfast. You'd been to Mass and when you took your hat off I could see the big black mark of the ashes on your forehead. I'd seen that often before but it frightened me on you. It terrified me. I could hardly swallow my coffee. Your forehead was so white with that make-up and that big dark smear . . . I can still feel the way my coffee stuck in my throat. It was as if I saw you dead . . . " Mike listened to all of this an said nothin at all but then he put out a hand an twined his fingurs inta Denis's where they rested on the urun. First I felt a kinda shock – like an electric shock. An then I felt a lot a love. Definitely a lot a love. An I realised that Mothur wasn't just campin it up when he was goin on about Mike. He loved him. He really did. I was amazed actually. But what was really very very surprising was that Mike wanted him too. I knew it. I could feel it.

The dansurs were goin like mad! They were flingin their shirts off an singin like crazy.

You can ring my be-e-ell!
You can ring my bell!

"But you looked very beautiful to me too . . . " Mothur was off again. A silence. He was starin at me. "Maybe next year I'll go into one of the Catholic churches on Ash Wednesday and get ashes on my forehead in memory of Tony . . . I don't know if I have the courage to do that."

"You can come with me," said Mike, smilin at last. "I always go on Ash Wednesday. Tis about the only time I go at all . . . "

"And then breakfast in Bewley's," said Mothur.

They sat there smilin at one anothur an I felt I shouldn't be there at all. This was so private. This was a Denis I didn't even know. I tried to turn my attention away, back to the dansurs, but I felt a kinda resistance an I had to come back. Twas like my job was to be there for them. I was almost shocked. This was a whole new role in life –

like as if now I was to be there for othur people. Their hands felt warm on me. And alive.

So they were all ringin bells an swingin their hips when the Garda raid happened. This was somethin that happened on an off an we were used to it. As I said, the Garda station was across the road but they nevur came near us for years. So we figured that someone must have started complainin or informin an they had to act on it like. They had to because twas unlicensed premises an what's more, like I said, twas a disused place we'd opened up so twas squattin too.

Twas a scream really. The Gardaí useta be really embarrassed raidin the place – I mean all these big sheepish country lads with thick accents. Like they say in the country: the kind that could put a foal in a mule for yeh. They didn't know what to do with us – I mean we weren't thugs or aggressive or anythin, only a bit a "I'll hit yeh with me handbag" kinda stuff – but we useta draw em out to the last.

"Jaysis, tis the Guards!" Four of um.

"What's goin on herre now?"

Everyone started scramblin around to get rid a their drinks, mostly sluggin em back an stickin the glasses undur the tables. Holy God, what was goin to happen to me? I felt as if someone would pick me up in their panic an put me on their head. The barrel a Murphy's disappeared from the bar like magic. We'd a grand plank for it on a ledge outside a winda. They nevur searched very hard anyway.

Dec an the othurs headed back to the table but there was no way we could get rid a all the pint glasses, some of em still half-full, an the whiskey-bottle an glasses. Mothur sat there as if he didn't give a shit an even started sippin his whiskey. I suppose that's why two of em headed for our table. The othur two went in behind the bar an started pokin around. Everyone was scatterin around us an as soon as the Gardaí moved away from the door they all started pourin out an down the stairs.

"Shit!" said Liam. "They're headin for us." But he kept on sluggin back the dregs a the pints.

One a the Guards was an oldur man, real thick-set – we knew him well – Sergeant O'Sullivan was his name. Yur typical country-man. His nickname was Lethil Weapon. Dec really fancies the othur one. He's about seven foot tall with that high colour in the face that they all have. His nickname was Fawlty Towurs. Dec was kinda tinklin at him now an preenin himself an the poor fella didn't know where to look.

"What'rre ou drrinkin therre now?"

"Coke, Sergeant," said Liam.

The Sergeant picked up one a the glasses an smelt it. Me heart was in me mouth, I tell yeh!

"Well, that's not Coke now as farr as I can tell. We've no chice but to take ou in." An he made the mistake a stretchin out a hand to Mad Mary.

"G'waay or I'll scratch yur eyes out!" screeched Mad Mary an started goin absolutely ape. The Sergeant hadn't touched hur at all. What happuned was *she threw* hurself at the Sergeant an they clung. The poor man looked absolutely desperate, holdin Mary's hands tryin to keep hur off.

"Now, Mary, Mary!" Mothur started haulin at Mary.

"Don't touch herr, don't touch herr whateverr ou do!" shouted Sullivan to Fawlty Towurs who was tryin to help him. "Jesus Chrrist! Arre ou dhrrunk or are ou dhrrugged?" he shouted at Mad Mary.

Next thing, while the Guards weren't lookin, Liam grabbed me up from the table an dived behind the Wizard a Oz scenury, a great big partition kinda thing – an Dec followed him. They were in hysterics an bitin their hands to keep quiet.

Next thing the partition started rockin.

"Stop leanin forward, yeh stupid bitch!" screeched Liam at Dec an the whole bloody thing collasped – right on top a Mothur an Mary and the two Guards an all. "Oh, Jaysis, now we've done it!" An they dived in past the bar an out the othur side an the way it is there's a scaffoldin kinda place, like an attic, ovur Whippins an Lashins an when yeh go through there yeh end up in the upstairs room a the Deaf an Dumb Association. Yeh havta squeeze yur way through the join in a kinda panellin – made a hardboard. We could hear the Guards followin us an then the scufflin at the panellin when they tried to bate their way through. They didn't see the join first.

The lights were on in the Deaf an Dumb but there was no-one at home. Down sat me two boyos at a table an when Lethil Weapon an Fawlty Towurs burst through they were signin away like mad – y'know, like deaf people.

For a start, the Sergeant was a bit put-out when he saw the damage he'd done to the panel – they were biggur than us, y'see, so when they pushed through they pulled out all the nails top an bottom an a bit of it had broken off in his hand. So he kinda looked up an down at it, not sayin anythin an his face was a picture.

Then when he started for us he stopped an stood there lookin uncertain. He knew twas them, a course, but you could see him thinkin a the fix he'd be in if by any chance he was makin a mistake an they actually *were* deaf an dumb people.

"Come an now, lads, that's enough of that now," he said. "Come quietly now and maybe I'll be able to do somethin forr you." An he stood there breathin hard like a bull. Honest to God, he was almost pawin the ground.

But Liam an Dec were havin a great time at this stage so they kept signin like mad as if they were amazed at the sight a the Guards.

"You'rre taking this too farr now – we'll have to place you underr arrrest," said Lethil but he still stood there.

"Ah hee yooking fo sohwa?" sayd Dec like the deaf wan on the telly – y'know – that programme with that *hunk* in it – the fella that sleeps with his dog – what a *waste*.

"Two fehas wen doh the stahs."

"Yerrrah, what'rre ou sayin at all?" said Lethil.

"Ah hou mockhin mhe?" says Dec. "Hi'll cohpain hou to houh supehiohs!"

Fawlty Towurs cleared his throat an stepped forward, all red in the face. "I'm placin ye under arrest."

"Oh, great," says Liam. "That means we get frisked." An me two boyos got up an turned their back to the Guards an leaned on the table with their legs stretched out an their butts in the air.

"Don't touch them whateverr ou do!" said Lethil Weapon – the voice of experience.

The lads didn't get frisked.

Back we went. Fawlty Towurs went through the gap in the panel first an Lethil Weapon waved the lads through as if they were two vehicles in a traffic jam.

"Jesus Christ!" Fawlty Towurs was swearin ahead a us as he blundered through the attic bangin his head agin the scaffoldin he was so tall.

"Let them get away an you'll answerr to me," said Lethil Weapon. "God wouldn't you luve to hit em a thump!"

"Don't even think of it, Sergeant," said Dec.

"We'd have it in tomarra's *Examinur*," said Liam. "I'm goin out with a fella in the *Examinur* office. Twould make a grand headline: Gay man beaten by Garda."

"Molested," said Dec. "Molested is better: Gay man molested by two Gardaí."

"Jaysis, maybe twould be worrth it!" said Lethil.

Tizzy was waitin for us back at the club an didn't he fall down the stairs head ovur heels on our way out. "I've no drink taken, Sergeant!"

When we got ovur to the Police Station only Mothur an Mad Mary were there, Mothur to hold Mary's hand – fair dues to him. I mean Mothur was well-known in the city but there he was, all ovur that creature. But Mothur nevur gave a shit. And the funny thing was, people always respected him. He could make yeh feel good about yurself like that, y'know?

No soonur were we in the door but this Ban-garda came up to Dec. "How are you, Declan?" she cried out, with a big delighted smile on hur face. "Look! Tis him! That I d'be tellin ye about! Tis Carmel!" An she threw an arm around him. The Gardaí all started cranin their heads from the office ovur the countur an around the door, to have a gandur at Dec.

"Have they moved yeh up from Union Quay?" asked Dec.

"Oh, tis just temporary! How are yeh at all at all?"

"I'm grand," says Dec, laughin.

"Will I evur forget it!" says she to the office at large. "The land we got when we found out he was a boy!"

"What's that?" asked one a the Guards.

"Two weeks he did up on the Western Road workin in a guest house dressed up as a girl – till the ownur attempted rape. Then he ended up in the Good Shepherds – told the nuns he was pregnant! How long ago was that now, Declan?"

"God, years ago – I was only fifteen!" Dec was usin the lovely gurglin voice I loved so much. "That was in a my willowy days!"

Twas always the way: Dec would tell yeh a wild story an yeh wouldn't believe it or yeh'd half believe it an then, soonur or latur, some Ban-garda or nun would come along an confirm it all. It got to the stage where I believed everythin he told me as a mattur a principle. Like he says himself: with all the things that happen to him all the time, why should he need to make anythin up? Actually, I'd met this Ban-garda before on an off around town when I was with him.

'Would ye like a cup a coffee?" asked the Ban-garda as if she was offerin the moon an the next thing we were all drinkin coffee – well, I wasn't – with the Gardaí. Mothur even sent Liam outside to bring Mike in – Mike was lurkin around waitin to see how Mothur got on.

When we came back in Dec was in full spate an all the Gardaí were grinnin their heads off.

"Carmel, says she to me, do you pad? Yes, says I. Your chest is very high, says she, wait an I'll fix it for yeh. An she started fiddlin with the straps of my bra. I was *amazed*. I had no idea you could do that! Like a little pulley!" Dec was gurglin away.

"But do tell us about the *rape* – yes!" said Denis. Denis could make a cup a lousy Gardaí economy-brand coffee look like a glass a champagne. That's what you call style, I suppose.

Dec laughed. "I saved my virtue by screaming out that I was goin to be a nun an that put him off – a religious man. But the housekeepur reported him and the Guards were called in. But I had taken off to the Good Shepherds at that stage an it took em days to find me. But let me tell ye – the first time he came to my room was hair-raising. He started telling me he was lonely, that his wife was away. I was very frightened because I knew what was going to happen. I knew he'd touch my breasts which were non-existent. I *froze*. So I wasn't prepared for what actually happened – he put his hand on my stomach and ran it down between my legs! Oh, I'm sorry, says he, I didn't know you were having your period!"

Even Lethil Weapon had a major eruption at that an hadta have one a his minions (Dec's word) wipe up the

coffee he spilt with his laughin. But then he musta realised
the fraternisin with the natives was aftur goin far enough.
He put down his cup, stuck out his chest, looked at us
from undur his bushy eyebrows an addressed the floor.
"Rright, lads," says he. "And yerrself, Mr Harte. I'm going to
let ye all off with a caution. The only thing I want to say to
you is: forr God's sake keep the drrink out of that club and
maybe we can let you alone . . . " The usual.

We went outside an stood around skittin about the raid
till they started feelin the cold an then we broke up. Mike
went off by himself down towards the bridge with his head
down an his hands in his pockets – or just the thumbs like
the covur of *Off the Wall*. Then Denis went off down
MacCurtain Street with Mad Mary hangin outa him as usual
an she havin fierce trouble with the heels.

"Dec?" Liam had somethin on his mind.

"Yeah?"

"I've been puttin it off like . . . I'd bettur go home."

Me heart gave a thump.

"But shur tis all hours a the night now . . . come back
with me, can't yeh?"

"Yayra, I'd say somebody would be up watchin telly.
Me mothur would probably be in bed but that's just as
well. Then I could tell hur in the mornin."

"Well, alright so . . . if that's what you want . . . "

Liam still stood there. "Dec?"

"Yeah?"

"I don't wanta take the urun home at all. I'd say me
mothur'd be upset about the cremation. I remembur she
heard Tony talkin about it once an she freaked – she said
you don't rise on the Last Day if you're cremated . . . "

"She may be right." With a sniff.

"Well, anyway, twould be bettur for me to tell hur
about the cremation latur – after she's ovur the first shock
like. So – could you mind Tony for me?"

Alright!

"Could you hang onta the urun like till we . . . "

Dec?

"Grand. No problem." An Liam handed me ovur. Dec stuck me in his bag. Right up agin somethin cold an stiff. An red. Yes, I could sense the colour in the dark. Is that so surprisin? I *am* a spirit, y'know. A greenhorn like, but a spirit all the same. I knew what the stiff red thing was anyway: this book about contemplative nuns with his collection a nun newspapur-cuttins stuck in between the pages. I lay there cursin the fuckin thing because I wanted to be on the othur side a it, pressed up agin his body. But then he closed his arm ovur me an I relaxed an started countin me blessins.

But not for long.

No rest for the wicked.

RIP, how are yeh.

We started up Summurhill. As Dec says, the hills were alive with the sound of music for all twas a miserable cold night in Cork – an twas my music. Liam had loaned him the Vangelis tape so Dec had shunted Joan Suthurland out of his Walkman. Wondurs will nevur cease.

Yeah! I thought.

No question I'm not alone –

Somehow I'll find my way home –

An there am I, God help us, on my high.

An then a car stopped.

"Can I give yeh a lift?"

I felt Dec tense up an hesitate. Then he relaxed an got into the car.

God Almighty. What now?

I knew what now.

I thought I knew.

The drivur was totally weird, like I mean he started talkin about this accident he had seen an he described loads a gore an blood an guts an things like that.

"Jesus! That's terrible!" says Dec.

The guy looked for all the world like yur man in *Taxi Drivur* – but oldur. He kept jerkin in his seat like as if he was helpin the car up the hill. I mean he was probably workin himself up.

"Mind the traffic," said Dec.

"Listen," says Taxi Drivur all of a sudden. "I'll give yeh twenty pounds to beat me."

What! I mean, yeh only hear about those things – yeh don't *do* them!

"No," says Dec. "I'm not into that kinda thing."

"Look, I won't lay a fingur on yeh! You just do it an I'll give yeh the twenty pounds straight inta yur hand an drive yeh home . . . "

Me heart hit the bottom a the urun. I could feel Dec waverin. He needed the money. Aftur handin over his dole to his mothur he wouldn't have a tossur for the week. Yur man begged an pleaded an in the end Dec said OK so like.

We got to his flat. I was in such a state I didn't know where we were. They undressed an Dec just stood there as if to say "What does he expect me to do?"

Taxi Drivur's langur was as miserable as the rest of him. He'd lost his hard-on in the cold – the flat was freezin – an I wished he'd get a jack again so his dick might look a bit more appetisin. As it was, twas turnin me stomach.

C'mere, this is a bit off the point now but don't yeh hate it when yeh're with some hunk an he takes off his trousurs an yeh're suddenly faced with yur little brothur? Don't yeh hate that? Don't yeh really hate that? An yeh have to pretend yeh still think he's Arnold Schwarzenegger? Be honest now! Don't yeh really hate that?

I do.

Not that I've evur *told* anyone that. Before. You'd be afraid a hurtin people's feelins. But I'm comin out since I became a spirit.

And it's not really off the point. Because . . . I dunno, it's hard to say this but . . . Well, I was really afraid to look at Dec, at his cock I mean. Yeh see, believe it or not, I'd nevur seen it before (what with *The Girls' Book a Piety* an all that) or if I had I was aftur forgettin what it was like. An . . . well, I was sayin to meself: what if it's a miserable effort like Taxi Drivur's? I was really afraid that . . . that I'd *lose* these great new feelins I was experiencin. That he wouldn't turn me on any more if he didn't have a decent cock. An, Jesus, then I'd despise meself. But there wouldn't be anythin I could do about it.

So I made meself look. An it was one a the hardest things I evur done in me life. And *God*, the *relief!* The sweat broke outa me. Yeah, it was gorgeous, as gorgeous as the rest a him and screamin out for my attention. Not so very long, y'know, but thick. I like thick.

Jesus, don't you just *love* cocks? Aren't they the coolest fuckin things?

Christ, I'm off again. Sorry. Sorry. Where was I?

Oh, yeah. The cold.

"Would you mind turning that fire on?" says Dec, readin me mind again. He didn't have a hard-on eithur, a course, but his dick had that kinda swollen bouncy look about it like it was thinkin a goin for one.

I was the only one with a hard-on an I didn't even have a dick. But with me, twas more like my whole soul was an erection, a feelin as much pain as pleasure let me tell yeh.

"The place is freezing," says Dec. "I can't function in this cold."

"Oh, right," said yur man an turned on the small electric fire – one bar. He musta been a misur with it.

"Do you mind if we have the two bars?" said Dec. "It really is very cold and I'm a bit consumptive."

"Oh, right," said yur man.

Next thing he opened his wardrobe an there was every kinda cane an birch an stick an whip inside.

Get the fuck outa here, Dec! Suddenly I wasn't this kinda engorged soul any more. I was shrunken an cold an full a fear.

"Oh, my God!" says Dec. "I hope yeh don't expect to use any of that on me!"

"No, no, like I told yeh, I just want yeh to do it." An he started strokin the things.

"Can I ask you a question?" Dec was bein real polite.

"Go ahead."

"Well – how did yeh start this thing?"

"Well, me fathur useta give me a hidin an that turned me on. An then it happened in school. I useta get inta trouble at school on purpose to get a hidin."

"D'yeh have any preference?" says Dec.

"A bamboo . . . "

So he hands Dec a bamboo an without more ado bends ovur an Dec just laced inta him. Twenty quids worth like. He stopped a couple a times an asked "Are yeh alright?" an yur man said "G'wan, g'wan!" An Dec went on layin inta him, skittin away like mad – good job he wasn't laughin in yur man's face like. Yur man was groanin so hard he probably couldn't hear him anyway. In the end yur man kinda doubled up an just jerked himself off in agony as far as I could see. Then he stopped moanin an knelt up again.

"Could you drop me home please?" says Dec.

He dropped us off at the library near Dec's.

"Goodbye," says Dec. "Thanks a lot."

I felt faint, I tell yeh.

So finally. The peace an calm a Dec's room. But I'd lost it. Twas all too much an me nerves were stretched to the last. I was in a ridiculous state a mind for a spirit. I'd nevur forgive him.

He tore off his clothes an slapped a cassette in his

playur. A bunch a nuns singin. I knew it well – he'd made me listen to it often enough (Listen to that! Isn't it *beautiful*! No, really listen to it now! Their voices are so *pure*!) The Adorurs of the Sacred Heart. Tyburn Convent.

Into the bed with us. I wasn't surprised. It seemed natural. I lay there against his chest listenin to his heart thumpin. Life.

I forgave him.

That heartbeat. *"For it is the drum of drums . . . "* I sang *Love-song for a Vampire* start to finish with the nuns goin *"Ora pro nobis! Ora pro nobis!"* It sounded grand.

The Tyburn Mix.

Twas a grand bed, the kind that dips in the middle. No fear a me rollin away from him. I was itchin to feel his skin – I could feel the softness a him but not the actual *feel* of his skin. The blissful feelin began to slip away. It was maddenin not to be able to touch him. I imagined how his skin would feel: soft, silky with just that tiny bit a stickiness an roughness so that it'd resist me cheek as I rubbed against it. I was thinkin a this ad for condoms I'd seen on telly – this ould codger with the monstur of a condom he called Geronimo – he'd had it for forty years or somethin. Like havin a bath in your sock he said it was. Well, that was me now. The urun was like a fuckin great big condom. Maybe I'd call it Geronimo. I rubbed against his nipple, the roughness of it strokin across that cheek I didn't have. I moved my imaginary head to an fro, rubbin my cheek ovur that nipple, till it got hardur an hardur an I could just turn my head an take it in my lips . . . Jesus! At this point I found meself fantasisin about the urun burstin open an me spillin out all ovur him – *I'm fallin like rain, I'm comin down around ya!* – or even him plungin his hands inta me an throwin me ovur him – in his hair, in his . . . Oh, Holy God, I was drivin meself mad!

I concentrated on the nuns, on the cool cool pure pure

voices. Even if I couldn't touch him I could smell him – I was lying there in that grand human man smell. So I made meself forget about touchin him an just breathed breathed him in till we were one an then I was in Heaven.

What a day! What an aftur-life!

Tizzy was an ole dote, alright. That langur from Dublin with his ten minutes before the train.

A bamboo.

"Dec," says I. "Stick to wankin. Yeh know what they say: yeh meet a bettur class a fella."

Don't think he heard me.

CHAPTER 3

NEXT MORNIN WAS DOLE MORNIN. WE WERE DOWN IN THE queue by half-nine. Liam was there tryin to get signed on.

Straight down to the The Long Valley for a pint. Two pints. Three pints. Inta the snug. Dec always liked a snug so he could chat to the ould women. Though in The Long Valley yeh're more likely to meet students from UCC or French tourists who've found it in their Michelin Guides.

By the way, don't get me wrong now. Tisn't a gay pub. Twas just handy like. An no, I'm not tellin yeh which are the gay pubs. An be sued for doin damage to their business? But there have always been gay pubs in Cork, all ovur the place. Like one up North Mainah an one up Barrackah an so on. They'd actually be *old* gay pubs – places where gay men have always gone for years an y'know found each othur on the sly an they would be camouflaged with ould wans drinkin (y'know the types, a glass a Murphy an a small whiskey – a pint an a drop). An now, a course, all the new places – packed full a trendy dykes talkin about k.d. lang's new album.

"What are we goin to do about Tony?" asked Liam when they were aftur lubricatin their brains an leavin the pub.

"Don't worry. Where there's a will there's a way. Climb

every mountain. And so on. *To dream the impossible dream, to fight the unbeatable foe . . .* " And he sang at the top of his voice all the way down Pana. Liam didn't take a tack a notice – he was used to it. So was I. Twas great. I'd a loved it if he'd done the quartet from *Rigoletto* but he needed me or Liz to do that – he had each of us trained to do two a the parts at the same time. With him doin the othur two. No, honest to God, it worked! Really!

When we got to Dec's house his mothur was a bit odd. Well, not just a bit odd – in real bad form. She was there with two a Majella's childrun an puttin up with the two a them whingin was drivin hur up the walls, she said. She took the dole money an didn't give him back anythin outa it eithur.

"There's a smell a drink off ye," says she. "At this time a the mornin!" An she kinda sniffed. "How did yur mothur take it, Liam?"

"Bad. Fierce bad. But she was alright before I left home. Dolores was makin her go up for a liedown."

Dolores is our sistur. But we always called her Drachma since the night the Greek ship came in an she went down an had a whale of a time an came home in the mornin with these thousands a drachma. Y'know: "Get up, get up! C'man, Tony! Liam! We're goin to the pub, get up, get up, we're goin down ta the bank – I'm aftur makin a fortune!" An we went down an she got eighteen pounds. She was disgusted.

"Twill be a long time before yur mothur's alright – shur she's heart-scalded from ye! And God only knows what's in store for us all . . . " Turnin the eyes to the Sacred Heart picture. "Jesus, Mary an Josuph! Tis no wondur there's neithur luck nor wealth in this house!"

There was a knock at the door. Twas the ould wan we'd met the day before. She had an empty cup in hur hand. I could just hear hur: Would yeh have e'er a bit a sugur?

"I'm up in me slippurs! How are yeh, Nuala?"

"I was just sayin, Mrs Burke, yeh'd put yur heart up on a plate for em an shit is yur thanks!"

Mrs Burke puckured hur lips an waited for more.

"Mrs Burke, we swagged an we hauled all our life an what thanks do we get for it? Used and abused! When I think of it – I could be up in the pub with the rest of em all these years. I coulda been ovur across the road in the pub passin bags a crisps out the door an money for ice-lollies for all the good it's done me! Come here an I'll pick yeh up!" The last bit was to the small wan, Sinéad, who was aftur comin into the room bawlin. "What happened to yeh? Did Conur hit yeh?" Sinéad nodded ferociously. "*Conur!*"

Conur came to the door.

"Come here, come here! What did yeh do to hur? Tell me an I won't hitcha."

"I didn't touch hur!"

"Mam," says Dec. "I think she just fell."

"Don't talk to me, you!"

"Wisha," said Mrs Burke. "Don't be so hard on him!"

"Hard on him! I'll be dug outa him one a these days!"

Dec struck a pose, hand on hip, an I knew he was goin to hold forth. "Mothur," says he. "*Your* mistake was not taking your cue from St Rita. 'Lord, I would rathur see my sons dead than see them stain their souls with sin!' Think of the courage a that! And her prayer answured and the two lads dead within the year! A hard woman! A *great* woman! Wouldn't it have been fittur for you to do that? I could be safely in my grave – "

"Don't, don't, *don't* start on Rita," said his mothur. "An *unnatural* bitch! God forgive me but she was! A *hardened* bitch! God forgive me!"

"Shur they were all hardened bitches if you like, Mothur. Look at The Little Flowur even – Little Block of

67

Granite her biographur said she should be called. Heroic Virtue, Mothur, it's called. Rita had her priorities right."

"Oh, Rita's great," put in Mrs Burke. "'Tis many a prayur she's answured for me. The Saint of the Impossible."

"She *earned* it," said Dec. "Eighteen years married to a total bastard before she could entur the Augustinians."

"And what happened to *him*?" Liam wanted to know.

"Murdured. Found murdured in the hills with his body gaping with daggur-wounds – "

Liam burst out laughin.

"*Lave* us *alone* about Rita!" said Mrs Leary.

Dec gave her a look an sashayed into the kitchen.

"Sit down, Liam," said Mrs Leary. She got out hur fags an lit up an gave Liam one. She gave a big sigh. "Poor Tony. Your poor mothur . . . " She took a long pull on hur fag. "I don't care if she *is* canonised! An *unnatural* bitch! Would yeh doubt Dec to fix on an unnatural bitch like that! He was nearly the death of me when he was young. *Thorns* he used to stick down his shirt – to be like Rita!"

"'Tis a pity he didn't last in the Brodurs, Nuala," said Mrs Burke. "He shoulda been a priest altogethur."

"Priest? Don't talk t'me!" said his mothur. "'Tis a queer crowd a priests we have nowadays – half of em nobburs! Aren't they in the papurs every day for child-abuse an worse. Will yeh look at yeh?" The last bit to Sinéad. "Dec, would yeh bring out the face-cloth there!"

"Nuala, would yeh have e'er a bit a sugur? Twould save me havin to go down to the shop . . . "

"Of course, Mrs Burke! Dec! The bag a sugur!"

"An could I have a look at the papur? I just want ta see if there's anybody dead . . . "

"Liam, hand Mrs Burke ovur the *Examinur* there – tis on the chair behind yeh . . . "

Dec came through with the face-cloth an the bag a sugur. He took the cup from Mrs Burke's hand an started fillin it with sugur.

"Thas grand, thas grand, oh thas too much entirely!"

"We've loads of it there." He heaped up the cup.

Mrs Leary started scrubbin Sinéad's face.

"I've raised me own an a thankless job it is an here I am now, stuck with Majella's!" Then she mouthed ovur Sinéad's head to Mrs Burke. "She's very crabbit. Oh, a right little madam! She'd run rings around Conur an he two years oldur than hur."

"Shur, the little boys d'be very innocent," said Mrs Burke with the dotin expression on hur face that goes with that sayin. "But the girls are madams from the day they're born."

"Isn't it true for yeh," said Mrs Leary as if she hadn't heard the same thing said hundreds a times before.

"D'yeh remembur Dec sittin out in the pram in those little knitted bonnets, Mrs Burke?" asked his mothur. "An the people passin in the street stoppin to look at him he was so pretty. I think a that now sometimes. Will yeh look at yer ears!" She started scrubbin Sinéad's ears.

"And, Nuala, the day yeh took him ovur to the Reparation to be consecrated to the Blessed Virgin an you laid him out on the altur in his Christenin robes with the blue shawl for Our Lady around him – oh, he was beautiful that day! I nevur saw such a beautiful baby!"

"And do you remembur, Mrs Burke," said Dec. "How we used to play weddings in your back garden and have a chalky god, a broken one, for a wedding-cake . . . "

"And you'd always be the bride," said Mrs Burke, laughin. "The innocence of it!"

Mrs Leary gave Dec an eye at that.

"Ah shur, Nuala, Dec's always been a great boy – weren't yeh lucky to have him an you out workin."

Dec had one a them absentee fathurs like them landlords in the history books, always comin an goin to

England. Till he finally stopped comin. An that was no harm because he drank an was violent an had the family up to its eyes in debt. So she always had to work an Dec was the one who cooked an coped as soon as he was able. They had a woman to take care a them until he was old enough to do it. If there was any swaggin and haulin done in that family twas Dec that done it.

"*I done it m-y-y wa-a-a-y!*" Dec burst out as soon as we left the house an it gave me a jolt – twas like an echo of what I was thinkin. "But y'know, those weddings – I'd always imagine I was marrying Peter Pan. That time I had a thing for him. And he was a cartoon! That's what bugs me to this day!"

Liam was laughin. He was beginnin to look much bettur altogethur. The kinda strained look around his eyes was goin an he looked youngur. "C'man an we get a video to take down ta Denis's!"

So: the usual row about what to take out. Liam wanted everythin an anythin from *Carravaggio* to *Terminator 2* but nothin would satisfy Dec. "Why not *The Song of Bernadette?*"

Tis always "Why not *The Song of Bernadette?*" If not that, tis "Why not *Debbie does Dallas?*" Whatevur that is – soft porn I think.

Just when I thought they'd end up gettin *Gone with the Wind* again they settled on *My Beautiful Launderette* – an the video joined me an the nuns in Dec's bag.

Next thing they decided to call in to see Cliona. Me heart sank to the bottom a me urun.

"I heard she's inta Guards these days," said Liam.

"What! Deserting our deserving clergy? Nevur!" said Dec. But we all knew she loves the Guards – she loves anythin kinda big an masculine an broad an she loves uniforms – not sailors now, they'd be little boys to hur – but she might go for the officurs. But, yeah, she loves the

Guards – half the time we suspected it might be hur callin the Guards to raid us – y'know, sayin there were drugs an that in the club. But priests were really it with hur – priests were the thing. Shur she even had this story that she was the offspring of a priest.

We got to hur flat. I was pissed off before we evur went in. The usual scene. She came out to the door in a T-shirt, a long one, an sugur-all else – we knew that because she flashed to show us what she didn't have on hur. With that big grin on hur face that always rubbed me up the wrong way. I misewell tell it to yeh straight – I nevur had time for Cliona. I didn't like her goings-on. I didn't like the way she took Dec ovur as if she owned him. I didn't like the fact he thought she was a hard case. I didn't like her messin with priests. I didn't like the fact she was a pushur. An a shopliftur. Call me old-fashioned if you like. Anyway, as far as I'm concerned, she's taboo.

In we went anyway an sure enough there was this priest sittin there – in his full regalia, mind you. I don't accuse him a doin anythin – apart from listenin to Cliona tellin him somethin like "I think I'm pregnant" or "I'm having a nervous breakdown" or "I'm in love with a priest but I can't tell you who he is." An gettin a jack watchin her flashin at him ovur on the couch.

"Hello, Fathur," said the lads, very respectful.

He kinda gave a half-grin an put his thumb-nail between his teeth.

They followed hur into the kitchen. She put the kettle on an got out the coffee.

"What're yeh doin with the Pillur a the Church?" asked Liam.

She mouthed a big "fuckin". She always lets on she's been fuckin um but I don't think that's true. I think, an Dec thinks, she lets em fondle hur breasts – that sorta thing. But yeh wouldn't know. I went one day to hur flat an there

71

was a fella runnin around in his undurpants an he was a priest too. I know him. There was somethin goin on that day alright. Dec thinks she has a frigid sorta problem an just likes to do this teasin thing. I dunno.

Anyway, she mouthed "fuckin", barin a mouthful a big long teeth. Everythin about hur is long, nose an all – she has a face like a horse for all the world. An the hair too – long an stringy – the numbur a times I've heard Tizzy say "Come in now durin de week an I'll give yeh a nice bob" but she nevur did. Mosta the time she looks like some kinda relic a the 70s with trailin skirts an shawls an beads. An everythin long. Except when she's at work when she's all prim an propur. Believe it or not, she's a doctur's receptionist. On the days she isn't out sick. Yeh know what I mean?

Jesus, don't let me go on any more about the woman. Tis a waste a breath.

I came to meself to hear Dec sayin: "D'yeh mean to say he isn't yer uncle? No? I'm *amazed*!" Everyone is Cliona's uncle – she has uncles right, left an centur. Some of em priests. Some of em in the Guards. "Shur, Annie Murphy is only trottin aftur yeh!"

The kettle was boilin. "Don't bothur makin any for us," said Dec. "Just attend to His Revurence – two sugar and two Dikanol crushed – and a chocolate bikky . . . "

Cliona started to shuffle round the kitchen. "I'm like a young wan!" says she to Dec in a high whinin Cork accent. "I'm up in me slippurs!"

"Yur hayur's lovely! Is it yur own?" Dec was off.

"No, tis me modur's!"

"Hey," said Liam, interruptin em thank God. "Have yeh been beaten up at all recently?" She was famous for it – y'know, the ould black-an-blue make-up an off with hur down to the Garda Station. She could put anythin ovur like. Brilliant, that way.

"Raped," said Cliona. "Laugh! Didn't the Ban-garda examine me and all and then the Sergeant came in with his little notebook. 'Tell me now – was there penethrrayshun?' Then he sent Fawlty to check out the Scayne a the Chrrime with me . . . "

"And was there penethrrayshun?" asked Dec.

Cliona pulled an I'm-not-tellin face an grabbin Dec an Liam, an arm of each of em, started side-steppin across the kitchen. Hur feet were bare an she had chilblains on hur small toes. Hur toes were as long as the rest of hur an ugly with it. There were goose-pimples on hur legs.

"*One, two, three, four, five,*
Fawlty Towurs ate me alive!
Six, seven, eight, nine, ten,
Liam is out of step again . . . "

Jesus! Talk about childish! Typical! The lads were gigglin like mad an that irritated me. She could be so fuckin stupid. The coffee was gettin cold on the countur. So was the Pillur a the Church in the sittin-room. I wished they'd remembur him.

He was wishin the same. There was a knock at the door.

"Deo Gratias!" Dec called out.

The Pillur stuck his head in, very sheepish. "I'd better be goin . . . "

"Oh, but I've just made coffee for you!" She grabbed up the mugs an followed him out, swingin hur behind.

Christ, Dec, let's go . . .

We went. "Right," said Dec. "We'll flake away from ye." He smiled at the Pillur. "Have a good day, Fathur."

"Oh," says Cliona. "Tell yeh what – meet ye latur ovur at the Funeral Parlour at the end a Shandon Street – five o'clock."

Me hackles rose, yeh could say. I could smell trouble.

"Who's dead belongin to yeh?" asked Dec.

"No, no – no-one. There's just somethin I want to do there . . . "

So they agreed to meet hur – fuckit – an, thanks be to God an His Blessed Mothur, we left.

I was so pissed off that I wasn't a bit pleased when Mad Mary opened the door to us at Denis's place.

"Holy Hour!" said Dec. "God between us an all harm! Wouldn't that put the heart across yeh!" An he started blessin himself like mad. Mad Mary was aftur gettin outa the drag gear an now was got up like a ravin punk in black leathur an safety pins an God knows what. Nose-rings. Nipple-rings. He'd spiked his hair – he musta spent the mornin at it. He'd taken off some a the make-up but had on loads a eye-linur an dark-red blackish lipstick. Jaysis, what do I mean he'd got outa drag?

"He's in dere," says Mary, pointin to the closed livin-room door, an lurched into the bedroom. He was still wearin the high heels.

"Cohen," said Dec. We could hear Leonard Cohen through the door, real gentle an sweet for once in his life:

You'll be hearing from me, baby, long after I'm gone.
I'll be speaking to you sweetly from a window in the
tower of song . . .

Liam knocked at the door.

"Come in!"

Denis was standin in fronta his easel, brush in hand.

The place was a wreck.

"Benedicite." Dec planked me down on a table aftur makin a space for me by pushin back all kinda shit with his hand. Then he circled slowly on his heel with his arms out an his eyes dilated, takin in the state a the room. "Unbelievable!" says he. "How can you live like this? Tell yeh what – I'll just scattur Tony's ashes round here at random. Twill make you and Cohen feel more at home an we'll save ourselves the expense of a funeral."

Denis stared. "Cohen? Oh . . . 'the ashes of the gay'." He
gave a very dry laugh. The hand with the paintbrush went
to his forehead ovur his eyes. "Declan, at times . . . "

"At times, what?"

"At times your sense of humour is – is – "

"Sick," said Liam.

"Thank you, Liam."

"'Morbid' is the correct word," said Dec. "You're calling
me morbid? And you listening to that ghoul . . . " He
pointed at Cohen in the hi-fi.

Give me crack and anal sex, sang Cohen,
Take the only tree that's left
And stuff it up the hole in your culture . . .

"Jesus Christ, will you listen to him?" said Dec. "Do we
really have to put up with that kind of thing?"

Liam was starin at Denis's canvas. "C'mere, Dec!" Dec
went ovur an stared too. I couldn't see, worse luck.

"I don't know about you at all, Denis," says he at last.
"You mean people will pay good money to put that on
their walls? Twould put me off my food."

"I like it," said Liam. "Tisn't a bit like Mary."

"Excuse me now," said Dec. "Tis *exactly* like Mary. Will
yeh look at the nose – an the knobbly knees – an the thick
ankles! That's a revolting pose, by the way, Denis – "

"Yeah, tis Mary," said Liam "But he's made him look . . .
I mean tis cool . . . it kinda hits yeh . . . "

Denis smiled very slightly at Liam – twas more with his
eyes – but I could tell he was really pleased. Then Liam
looked pleased too. I was itchin to see the picture. Like I
wanted to have me say, y'know? An to see if Mary'd got a
ring put on his cock. I suppose they'd have made some
kinda crack about it if he had.

"Well, in my humble opinion – an I know I'm no art-
critic like – the back a the fire is the place for that," said
Dec.

When they said repent! Repeeent!
I wonder what they meant?
Cohen was goin ape.

"Will yeh listen to him?" said Dec. "Is that the same fella that said he'd be singin to us sweetly from a window in the Tower of Song while ago? Jesus, he must have a megaphone!" Denis laughed at this.

"Seriously, why not Joan Suthurland?" asked Dec.

"We can have Aretha Franklin – if you want a lady with soul," said Mothur.

"Give me Maria Callas any day," said Dec.

Denis got suddenly impatient. He waved us away. "Daahlings! Go make yourselves some coffee!"

In comes Mad Mary on cue with coffee for Denis.

"Oh, making yourself *useful*!" said Dec to him. "But would it nevur occur to you to clean up this . . . this disastur-zone!"

"Fuck aaafff, baaoy!" said Mad Mary an Liam togethur.

"I don't know about you at all, Denis," said Dec but his eyes were fixed on Mary. "How you can bear lookin at that scrawny chest . . . to say nothin of paintin it!"

Mary was wearin his leathur jacket without a shirt or vest.

"And he'll have yur eye out with that nose some night!"

"Look, look," said Denis. "I need to get some work done, children! Go squabble in the kitchen or fuck yourselves in the bedroom or whatever – just don't talk to me!"

"We've got a video," said Liam. "*My Beautiful Launderette.* Daniel Day Lewis."

"Oh, *damn*!" said Mothur. "I want to see that!" And he threw down his brush.

"I'll work away," said Dec. "I'll be keeping half an eye on it. Get it out of the bag, Liam." An he started collectin all the used mugs an glasses around the place.

Next thing there was a howl from Liam. "*Deeeec!* Yeh stupid bitch! Yeh stupid mothurfuckin cunt!" An he started jumpin around, beltin his feet off the floor in a rage.

Mothur an Mary stared. "Whatever is the matter, darling?" asked Mothur.

"The stupid mothurfuckin bitch got out the *Song a Bernafuckindette!*"

"Hand me ovur that glass there, Liam," says Dec, stretchin out a hand.

Liam picked up the glass an hefted it in his hand, lookin dangerous. "Jay, stay well away from me or I'll put it a place a prick nevur hit!"

Dec posed brazenly with his head to one side an a hand on his hip – the othur was bristlin with mugs. "I've lost you now, Liam – isn't that the video we decided on?"

"Yeh stupid git! You know what we fuckin decided on! *My Beautiful Launderette!*"

"Oh," said Dec. "I could have sworn you said *The Song of Bernadette.*"

Denis burst out laughin an Mary joined him a course, cacklin like crazy.

"Puss is aan anyway, baaooy!" said Mad Mary. "Whass iss abouss?" Hissin away on the ends a the words in the real Cork way.

"Our Lady a Lourdes." Liam, deadly quiet, eyein Dec.

Mothur went back to his easel grinnin away. "Do put it on, Liam! It *is* supposed to be a classic."

Mary grabbed it from Liam, slammed it inta the machine, pressed play an fell off his heels onta the sofa.

"Oh Gaaawd!" he screeched. "Tis blackinwhisse!"

The syrupy filum music filled the room.

Liam let a long sigh outa him an calmed down. "Push up in the bed, Mary," said he, haulin up Mary's legs an sittin on the sofa with Mary's legs on his lap. He took off the high heels. Mary's feet looked pretty raw. "I'll give yeh a foot massage."

"Make a good job of it, do," said Dec. "Give him a blow-job altogethur while you're at it."

"Nothing incestuous now, children," said Mothur.

So we watched the filum. Mothur painted. Dec cleaned up like mad an watched the filum at the same time, sayin things like "Isn't she *beautiful*! Isn't she gorgeous!" She was beautiful but she had a prissy little voice that drove me spare. Dec an Mothur got into an argument because Mothur said Our Lady looked like a Hollywood tart. Mad Mary thought Our Lady looked "gaargeous". When it was time for Dec to hoovur he hoovured an when he finished the room he went off to do the rest a the flat an only stuck his head round the door now an again or sashayed past the door – always with somethin different in his hand like tile polish or Windowlene or Pledge – he'd be shinin an polishin and so on. I was sorry I couldn't watch him at it. It always gave me a nice feelin.

"Tell me – how d'yeh expect me to clean?' says he at one point. "You don't have a drop of disinfectant of any kind in the house."

"I'm environmentally friendly, dahling," said Mothur. "I can't bring myself to buy that stuff. Those defenceless little microbes – it pains me to see those horrifically murderous commercials. Such savagery!"

"I'll bear the guilt," says Dec. Back into the kitchen.

Aftur a fair while Liam got a bit restless, shiftin around an givin little quick looks back to where Mothur was. Twas easy to guess the bit a pressure an friction – of Mary's legs on his lap I mean – was doin its work. I knew twas only because Dec was in an out that he hadn't his hand in the black leathur pants already. The thought had no soonur crossed me mind when he grabbed Mary's groin an to my disgust I must say – I didn't much like being a witness to this – they started developin a bit of a rhythm – very small an quiet but definitely a rhythm.

What Mothur had said about incest was right – I mean you wouldn't get off, or Gett Off to be funky like, with any a the lads. Maybe like in the early days that's how you'd meet someone but once you'd become friends – well, really, you'd be mortified. You wouldn't be able to do anythin anyway – you'd be laughin like. Except there's a sorta orgy scene an that'd be alright because it's not the same as beddin the one like an you'd all be out of yur brains anyway for that. What I want to say anyway is that nobody felt the same about Mad Mary – everybody used him up to the eyeballs all the time – like Denis was doin. That was because he's such a total flah-bag, a right hoor. Shur they used to drag Mary down to the STD clinic now an then an make him have a HIV test whether he wanted it or not – he always had a valid certificate – like a dog licence. I mean as far as those things can be valid, what with the question a time-lapse an all. Then immediately aftur the test he'd be really in business for a while. Makin hay while the sun shined. Twas only a mattur a time. An why Denis wasn't scared shitless a touchin him was a mystery. Why he *wanted* to touch him was anothur mystery. I'd say twas strictly a blow-job effort, though twas hard to imagine that with em sleepin togethur for so long. I dunno. Tis hard to figure people out sometimes.

Me two boyos were really enjoyin *The Song a Bernadette*. They were transfixed.

"Do you know Liam is taking liberties with your fiancée?" There was Dec with his cloth an window-spray. The two on the sofa got a right start. I wondured whethur things had come to a head, y'know what I mean? That would be alright for Liam with his blue jeans – nothin bettur than the ould denims for that kinda job – but Mary's leathur – well, it doesn't bear thinkin about. This fella I was jaggin with in England had leathur once an when it came to comin twas a disastur. He managed to sell em off second-hand – "as new".

Dec was carryin on. "She's a shameless huzzy, do you know that?" Mothur was lookin daggurs at him. I knew twas because a the fiancée bit. He wouldn't like that in case it gave Mary any ideas. There was always Mike, y'see, in the back a his mind. "An a conniving bitch as well – I know she wheedles money out of you – apart from the usual up-front payment."

"Ah," says Liam. "Though there's dough there there's love there too though. Isn't that right, Mary? Say it, Mary – say it for me, there's a good girl!"

"Ah, lave us alone," says Mary, real coy.

"Ah, go on, Mary! For me." A little bit a action on the nipple-ring. "Though there's love there . . . "

"Lemme alone, Leeem! Ya only wanta laugh ass me!"

"Ah, g'wan, Mary!" He slipped an arm around Mary's shouldurs an pulled him up so they were face to face. "Though there's love there . . . "

"Dough dere's dough dere dere's love dere too dough," says Mary in a rush. The reason why Mary had the cop-on to twig that this was a joke was because twas anothur old Cork one. Liam laughed outright in delight. It did me good to hear him sound happy. He started playin with Mary as if he were a Barbie doll – pullin at the hair-spikes an the earrings an the nose-ring an the nipple-ring an anythin else he could get his hands on.

Meanwhile Dec was inta the video an he was away.

"Oh! Isn't she beautiful?" Bernadette was in the nuns at this stage. Dec sat down on the armrest of a chair, starin at the screen. His face was all lit up, eyes shinin. I've seen him look like that at me even, once or twice. Once I remembur he looked at me like that an threw his arms around me. An he wasn't outa his brain at the time either – he'd had a few drinks like. "God, I really love you!" he said. I knew he meant . . . well, I dunno what he meant. Mind yeh, I'd seen him do the same with Liz. I wished he'd do it to me now.

I started thinkin about the night before. An how great it was. Twas different to what I was used to. I started tryin to figure out why but Dec was off again.

"*Why* can't they get someone in Hollywood to take them into a *real* convent. Now this is not bad but that bitch is unreal. I'm not sayin nuns can't be bitches – oh, God, I've crossed swords with some rare bitches in my time – like that wan up in the Bons – talk about powur-mad! The poor unfortunates working there – she useta lave em for dead. That's how I lost that job there. She useta make me clean the floor twice ovur – *she useta walk ovur it hurself* after I'd washed it an then turn round an tell me it was filthy. You wouldn't mind if I was a novice! God, she hated my guts! Well, one day I faced hur – oh tis very easy to humble a nun when they're on their high-horse. 'How dare you,' says I. 'If you think, just because you're a nun, I'm going to let a *jade* like you . . . '" He stopped short because Denis had come ovur an gripped him by a shouldur from behind.

"Declan, my lovely," said Mothur slowly. "You are spoiling the *pathos* of the film which you yourself have *inflicted* on us. Bernadette is dying of some monstrous tumour. Meanwhile I am trying to work. Could you be a good boy and either go back to the kitchen or *watch the bloody film.*" Then he got distracted an started eyein the arrangement on the sofa which he hadn't actually laid eyes on up to that. An eyebrow went up – he has a way a doin that, as if the eyebrow has a life of its own. Twas hard to read his expression though. He went back to his work.

Dec did a little camp shruggin thing he's good at. He shut up but not for long. "At least they have the veils on more or less right. Sisturs of Nevers. Isn't that veil just *beautiful? Look* at the wimple! The way it frames the face! There's nothing more flattering for a woman! They look so *beautiful* in it! Why any woman would evur want to dress any othur way is beyond me! Why any woman would want to *be* anything else is beyond me!"

"A bit hypocritical of you, darling," put in Mothur.

"*But* if I'd been a girl, y'know, I wouldn't have had to be a trollop." He really believed that. Could be right. "If I'd been a girl I'd be down in Glencairn with the Cistercians." He had his soft voice on that made me want to . . . put my arms around him.

"How about the Good Shepherds?" asked Liam. "Wouldn't yeh like that crowd?"

Dec stared at him. But like he was thinkin a somethin else.

"Whasupitcha, girl?" asked Liam.

But Bernadette was dyin at this stage: "I *did* see the Lady!"

Dec waved at Liam to shut up. An he sat there lookin like an anjul with his blue eyes shinin with tears.

CHAPTER 4

ON THE WAY BACK HOME DEC SAID HE'D AN IDEA ABOUT ME funeral but he refused to tell Liam what it was. But when we got there twas clear enough.

"Oh, God, no, Dec!" Liam was serious. "I'd be in terrur!"

But Dec was already in his navy skirt an was strugglin with his tights. "Give us a hand!" says he, annoyed. "Wait! No, keep well away from me with those filthy talons! A laddur an I'm banjaxed. The price of tights is atrocious these days."

It felt weird watchin Liam helpin him with the bra an the paddin. I'd done that job meself so often. Many's the time. The shirt. The flat shoes. The cardigan. The silvur crucifix around his neck. The silvur ring with the cross on his fingur: Bride a Christ. An the short veil he'd snaffled from Sistur Breeda.

Yeah, he really would've got a kick outa the old habit. If any of em wore em any more. An it broke his heart that they were all goin about in their sling-backs now. An he useta go to all the convents an visit – just to see these people livin an functionin an movin around. I remembur hangin ovur many a wall watchin nuns with their habits hitched up doin gardens. Monks, too, a course. But the nuns were the thing for him.

I got transferred inta a navy shouldur-bag of his

mothur's with his othur junk includin the nuns.

You'd always be a bit nervous when Dec was doin his thing in the habit even though we knew of old that it worked grand. He looked perfect. The blue eyes an the nice skin with a bit of pink in the cheeks made him look like an anjul if he wanted to start lookin like an anjul – he could turn it on. But the thing was, y'see, he knew how to look like a nun – not like those crap Hollywood wans that looked like chalky gods but like the real nuns you'd see walkin around. The way he'd move his hands an walk an climb a stairs an especially the voice an the laugh – well, I can't really say what it was but twas perfect anyway. Method actin. Like Al Pacino an them.

But, chalk it down, I wasn't turned on by Dec in drag. I've nevur been inta transvestites – well, in the sense I've nevur been enthusiastic about em. Though Mary's suspendurs, mind yeh, have a certain je-ne-hows-your-French about em.

Right, I wanted to get that across to yeh. I liked Dec in his own jeans an jackets an things, as himself, an not as some fantasy thing. But I could undurstand the buzz that was in it for him like. An that when he was in his nun's gear he was happy, feelin powurful bein his own creation like Ru Paul says.

Anyway, we were useta it.

So up with us to the Good Shepherds again. I was nervous. I knew this was anothur "recce" but I couldn't be sure they wouldn't get fed up with the whole capur if things went against em an maybe just pitch me into the Lee. Wouldn't blame em.

Me heart was set on anothur night with Dec. While we were walkin up Sunday's Well I was thinkin about the night before. So hard I wasn't listenin to the lads even. I figured out at last what was so great about it. The thing was, when I was in the flesh, if I'd a session like that, I'd be concentratin on what was happenin with me dick, like. I mean twould be all about worryin about gettin it up an keepin it up an not comin too fast and not comin too slow – or just gettin his hand or his mouth on it as fast as possible an gettin jacked off fast one way or the othur. But now I didn't have a dick to worry about an it was like I was gettin turned on all ovur me body an I kinda wanted to get all ovur *his* body an what I missed was me hands an me mouth. It was definitely diffurent. Twas great.

When I came outa this Liam was talkin. "So if twasn't him, who was it? Yur first time, I mean."

"A neighbour. Married. I musta been eight years old. He'd call you to go on a message, whethur you were a boy or a girl. If he tried anything on the othur kids they ran away. But he turned me on. We did a numbur of things. I didn't know what to be doing but he knew. Exploration. Touching. At the start. I didn't know anything about French kissing, even. I didn't know about jerking off. But he taught me all that. I liked it. I loved it. I knew I was very turned on. I was very relaxed about everything. I *wanted* what was happening to me to happen."

They went silent for a while. When Dec spoke again his voice was kinda hushed. "I can still feel that man's hands on me. They were warm. And his mouth. His lips were dry and warm – like his dick. I can remembur." They said nothin for a while. Then he spoke up again. "To this day what I really like is blow-jobs – giving them. That's what I like more than anything."

Twas really weird hearin all a this out of a nun, I tell yeh. Though I'd heard it all before.

"I don't have any problems about it," he went on. "I don't look back in angur. And say why didn't they leave me alone. I just don't. I mean I don't think they *done* it to me. I mean I was with him because I wanted it. Like I'd been waiting for it."

"Twas the same with me," said Liam. His voice sounded kinda strained. "A neighbour. Tis always a neighbour or a brothur or a teachur – that kinda thing, isn't it? I useta call him Uncle Brian. He was in his late fifties. He useta go for a lie-down in the afturnoons an bring me with him. He nevur tried to screw me or touch me that way at all but he useta kiss me. And I mean I was aroused. But like you said – I wanted it. I went back again an again I liked it so much. An like you said, I don't think anyone *done* it to me."

"Take it easy on the steps, will yeh – Our Lady was nevur seen taking two steps at a time."

An Liam started arguin about Our Lady an steps. So much for the heartfelt confessions.

Ten minutes aftur, we were havin tea with the Reverend Mothur. Dec had marched right in there – march is the wrong word for the way he was walkin – an told em he was home on holiday from Australia an Liam was his cousin.

He was terrific. Sittin there with his ankles togethur an his hands clasped in his lap. The little strands a hair across his forehead looked just right.

The Reverend Mothur looked like a man. She was tall an flat-chested with big heavy bones an wide shouldurs an a big hooked nose she kept blowin inta a handkurchief all the time. Then she'd cough an clear hur throat an spit somethin into the handkurchief. I tell yeh twas gross. An twasn't as if she was dyin from a cold. I mean hur eyes weren't streamin or anythin. She had chilly blue eyes like a fish an a smile they coulda used in *Dracula*.

There was anothur nun there too – Mothur Ursula – an she was the exact opposite. She was all round an hearty an red in the face with a big beamin smile, laughin all the time an all ovur Liam, holdin his hand in hurs. We finished our tea an then they took us to see Little Nellie's room. It had a small little white bed with a wooden armchair an a statue a the Infant a Prague in a glass covur on the cupboard – with his one ball, like Tizzy, in his hand.

"This is where she died," said the Bride a Frankenstein. She had a cracklin powurful voice. "Four years old, she was."

"Oh, isn't it lovely," sighed Dec. "It's so simple. An look at her toys!" A bunny-rabbit an a tin bugle.

"That's the statue that used to dance for her," said Mothur Ursula who was still hangin onta Liam's hand an kinda slappin the back of it from time to time for no reason at all. She was beamin at him an even strokin his face and sometimes even kinda butted his head with hurs. "She used to play her little trumpet and say 'Now little Jesus, dance for me!' And one of the Sisters said 'Dear Lord, if you really did dance for Little Nellie, give us money for a bakehouse which we badly need.' And a few days later a lady sent £300 with a note saying 'For a bakehouse.'" Hur teeth were big and white.

Dec was entranced. "So she was an orphan?" He knew it all a course already.

"Her mother died of consumption, Sister," said the Bride and, oh my God, the handkurchief came out again – outa the sleeve a hur cardigan. "Mrs Organ was her name. She clung to Nellie so hard at the end that the child had to be torn – torn, Sister – rudely, from her dying embrace." An she blew really hard into the handkurchief. It was drivin me spare, I tell yeh. Then we all waited while she cleared hur throat grossly an spat into the handkurchief. "So Nellie's father was left with four motherless children. Thomas was sent to the Christian Brothers, David to the Sisters of Mercy and Mary and Nellie came here."

We went on to the chapel where Nellie received hur First Holy Communion. There was a shrine to the Mothur a Perpetual Succour. Jesus had one sandal hangin off. I heard

Dec sayin "Jesus, wouldn't yeh think she'd tie the child's shoe . . . " and when I looked at him in shock I realised he hadn't spoken at all. He was just gazin at the picture in bliss like. But I'd heard him say it all the same. Things were lookin up. Definitely.

We went out to the grave with Mothur Ursula still hangin onta Liam an askin him all kinds a questions about himself that he didn't know how to answur.

"Well, Sister," said the Bride. "We're delighted to see you here." An she hit Dec a belt of hur hand, a kind of a slap on the back that sent a jolt through me. A big heavy white hand – you could see the powur in it when she kinda flicked hur wrist.

"Well, I'm here for a reason, Mothur," said Dec. "Not just a visit."

The Bride's eyes swivelled towards him ovur the handkurchief. Yeah, she was snortin into the handkurchief again. I'd a bit of a fantasy for a moment. The cold eyes without lashes were starin down the barrel of my Magnum 45 – the biggest gun in the world not mounted on a battleship – an I was sayin "You're wonderin whethur to take the risk an spit into that handkurchief again. Well, what you havta ask yurself is: Do I feel lucky? Well, *do you, punk?*" She spat an I blew hur away.

"So my hope is that he can have his wish . . . "

"The poor creature," said Ursula. "To die so far from home – and so young!" She caught Liam's hands togethur an kinda shook him like a puppy-dog. He musta been gettin useta it by this time.

"Does it run in the family?" the Bride was askin.
What!!!

"I'm afraid so," answured Dec. "My grandmothur went the same way and his own poor mothur, God help her."

"And could nothing be done, Sister?" asked Ursula.

"Some cases don't respond," answured Dec.

What had he told them? I'd missed it.

"*Well*, I think . . . in the circumstances . . . " said the Bride. "We can hardly refuse . . . "

"Oh, thank you, thank you, Mothur!" Dec's face was shinin. He kinda crossed his hands on his chest an did a little jigettyjig thing as if he was restrainin himself from throwin his arms around the Bride. "That's such a weight off my mind."

"Yes, but there's the problem of the fact that he was cremated," said the Bride, treatin us to a new trick – twirlin a two-tooth denture around in hur mouth. "I'm not at all sure that's acceptable – I know it wasn't in the past . . . "

"Oh, that ruling has been rescinded," said Dec. I knew he'd no idea whethur it was "rescinded" or not, whatevur "rescinded" means – changed, I suppose. "Not that I approve of it myself! I think it's opposed to human instinct and the better sentiments of the human heart."

The Bride looked impressed. The denture was spinnin like mad.

"It's a pagan practice after all," said Dec. "Minucius Felix spoke out against it in the third century."

Now the Bride looked *very* impressed. "I feel myself that Christian reverence for the dead protests against it," says she, not to be outdone, an very genteel through the nose. "Filial piety, for example, must be outraged at such treatment of, let's say, a deceased mother."

"Yes," said Ursula, gettin hur spoke in. "After all, the body is the Temple of the Holy Spirit and it should be allowed to rot away in God's earth according to the laws of nature, I always say. But what does Liam think?"

Liam looked upset and, I dunno, a bit bittur. I wondured what he was thinkin exactly.

Dec came to his rescue. "To say nothing of the medico-legal aspects."

They looked at him.

"Exhumation," said Dec. "For the detection of crime."

The Bride an Ursula were silenced by this expertise.

"I'll inform the Chaplain," said the Bride.

"If you don't mind, Reverend Mothur, he had a friend a Benedictine and I'd like him to officiate," said Dec. I could see Liam lookin at him with an expression on him as if he'd just sucked a lemon. I didn't have any friend a Benedictine. An actually, he didn't say Benedictine – but I'm callin him that now to confuse the issue. Yeh'll see why latur.

"Certainly, Sister," said the Bride.

"How many people do you expect?" Ursula wanted to know, all hearty. "We must give them a cup of tea at least! With Reverend Mother's permission . . . " An she looked at the Bride with hur head cocked to one side an the big toothy smile on hur face.

The Bride smiled a smile like a goose walkin ovur yur grave. "Of course," she said, grabbin Dec by the shouldur with hur big strong fingurs. I could feel him kinda wince. The woman didn't know hur own strength.

"Well, there would be ten at the most, I'd imagine," said Dec. "But I can confirm that latur."

Liam looked sick.

We finally got away down the drive. Liam said nothin till we hit the road. Then he started his jumpin up an down an cursin an swearin act. Dec let him at it. By the time we'd reached the rivur Liam had calmed down with the help of a couple a fags. He came up level.

"*What* are we doin all this for? All we havta do is go up an scattur the ashes an tis done! Say a few prayurs if yeh like! You're on a roll now an there's no stoppin yeh!"

"Calm yourself, my child." Dame Veronica was back. "Take the discipline tonight, the nine-thonged one, and pray for steadiness and control. I know you'll say it doesn't really hurt but I believe if you dip it in hot wax it's vastly improved. But use it only where one whacks small boys. And only for as long as it takes to recite one decade of the rosary. Masochism. Approved by the Church. But we mustn't take it too far. *Do* you understand?"

Liam threw his fag away, shook his head an gave up.

We'd got as far as North Gate Bridge before I rembured we were to meet Cliona, oh God, there at the Funeral Parlour at the back a the little square where Shandon Street meets the quay.

In with us. There were piles a people millin around at the back but the first thing we saw was Cliona kneelin by a coffin just inside the door with a black hat on hur an a veil back off hur face an she cryin hur eyes out. Cliona – that we'd last seen in a T-shirt flashin at a priest. The woman was sick. Off hur chuck.

The ownur or what would you call him was standin nearby lookin very concerned.

Dec went up an put a hand on Cliona's shouldur.

"Did they let you come by yourself?" says he, real surprised. "Where are the othurs?"

Cliona looked up. Fair fucks to hur, she didn't miss a beat. "Oh, Sistur!" she burst out.

They were away. God only knew what would happen now.

"Where are Paddy and Seán?" asked Dec. "And Séamus?"

"I don't know," Cliona sobbed inta Dec's skirt. "They closed the door in me face!"

"God forgive them," said Dec as if he really meant it. "Did you not see hur then? Before she went?"

"No," cried Cliona. "They wouldn't let me. I got Fathur Tom to speak to them. She's yeer sistur too, says he, an yeer mothur's daughtur whethur ye've acknowledged hur or not an now's yeer chance to make up for yeer lack of charity. Wouldn't ye do it for yeer mothur's sake an let hur

die in peace knowin she's been forgiven? Twas no good –
they wouldn't let me near hur."

"That's terrible," said Dec. "But what you should feel
now . . . " He stopped, starin into the coffin.

Cliona looked up at him.

"Shur that's not your mothur," said Dec.

"What?" said Cliona, gettin to hur feet. She stared at the
corpse.

"It's not your mothur," said Dec.

"It's not me mothur," screeched Cliona. She swung
round on the ownur. "You said twas me mothur!"

The poor man looked shocked. "Mrs O'Brien, didn't you
say? That's Mrs O'Brien . . . "

Cliona an Dec started goin about lookin inta the othur
coffins. "She's not here, she's not here at all!" Cliona was
sobbin. Everyone in the funeral home was starin.

The ownur was followin them with his face all splotchy
in his fright. "If there's been a mix-up, I'm sure it can be
sorted out . . . " He sounded strangled as if somethin was
stickin in his throat.

"Where's me mothur?" Cliona was wailin.

"Look, we'll wait for Séamus and the othurs to come
and we'll sort it out . . . "

"Oh, Holy God an His Blessed Mothur!" Cliona burst
out. "They've buried hur already without me, God forgive
them!" She started bawlin. "Oh, God! Oh, God!" An she
kinda staggured outa the funeral home with Dec an Liam
aftur hur. An everybody else too. They all crowded through
the doorway. She was down on hur knees in the street
now. She had taken the black hat off an was flakin it on
the ground. People were gatherin on the street. Liam's eyes
were startin from his head an his breath was comin hard.
He was scared. Even Dec was beginnin to look alarmed.
Cliona could take this all the way. An epileptic fit would be
the next thing now an we'd all be off to the hospital in the

ambulance. Or down to Union Quay in the Squad car.

No soonur did I think this than I heard the ownur say that he was callin an ambulance an he dashed inside.

Dec made as if to go aftur him but just then Cliona got to hur feet an stood there staggerin with the hat an veil in hur hand. An then before we knew what hit us she took off at a run – straight across the road, up onta the wall a the quay an with a fierce scream she threw hurself inta the rivur.

"Jesus Christ!" said Liam. "The mad bitch!"

When we got to the wall she was still screamin an flounderin around in the watur.

"Low tide," muttured Dec to Liam. "Naturally. She uses the Almanac."

"Jesus, the stupid bitch!" Liam was almost cryin. "What are we supposed to do now?"

"You jump in an get her," said Dec.

"Me jump in! Are yeh mad! I'm only sorry she isn't drownin!"

"We've got to get her out," said Dec.

"Well, jump in yurself!"

"How can I, dressed like this?" Fuckin right. An he had me to take care of, what's more. I had no intention a endin up at the bottom a that filthy rivur.

A small ould wan with a pink an purple hat grabbed Liam by the arm. "Jump in! Jump in!" she started shriekin. "Can't yeh jump in an save yur sistur!"

"Me sistur?" said Liam an he tryin to pull away from hur grip. "*That's* not me sistur!"

A man was startin to climb down the iron laddur into the rivur.

"Go ovur to the laddur!" Dec started shoutin to Cliona but she was too busy with hur drownin act to hear him.

"Wait! Wait!" someone yelled. "The Squad car's comin!"

The Squad car came down Shandon Street, the door

burst open an Fawlty jumped out. He took the situation in at a glance, as they say, an pulled his jacket off an then his shoes while he was runnin ovur to the quay-wall. Man of Action. Supurhero. His partnur was trailin along behind – not so keen . . .

Inta the rivur with Fawlty.

The usual. She grabbed him round the neck like she'd seen in all the good (and bad) comedies an dragged him undur. Ugh! The filth a that rivur!

"Hit hur ovur the head with yur truncheon," shouted Liam. A big gasp came from all the people around us an they looked daggurs at Liam.

"No?" said Dec. "More's the pity."

Fawlty had started to drag hur towards the laddur.

She began to come quietly, all wrapped around Fawlty.

The ambulance arrived, sirens an all.

They climbed the laddur. Or he did, haulin hur aftur him. The people were all clappin an cheerin – an laughin by this time. But they didn't really start laughin till Fawlty started to look for the Squad car. Twas gone. So was his jacket. An his shoes. The poor eejit stood there gaspin, with Cliona around his neck, starin around him like he'd found himself in his worst nightmare. He'd lost his fuckin Squad car. Yes! His partnur was even more stupified, if that's possible. Somebody's idea of a bit a craic, I suppose – I mean twas probably parked round the cornur. Who'd be eejit enough to steal a Squad car?

Dec an Liam decided to get the hell outa it. We crossed Northgate Bridge at a trot. Last thing we saw was Cliona an Fawlty bein helped into the ambulance.

"Stomach-pump," gasped Dec. "Both of em."

"You should know," said Liam. Like I said, Dec had been in an out a that rivur a fair few times.

Dec was still gigglin when we were walkin up to Denis's place. It felt great, walkin along with him giddy with laughin like I'd done so many times before. Every time he'd giggle I'd giggle with him an that seemed to make him worse. Then Liam would start laughin at Dec. It got to be a kind of a game. Then when he was really bad I'd say "That's not me mothur!" an he'd get really helpless. People were lookin at us strange. Somehow, the kinda communication between us was very sexy.

Denis was there on his own when we got to his place. He just raised an eyebrow at Dec's gear. He was cookin in the kitchen an paintin in the livin-room at the same time. He was in the middle a havin a bath too because he was all wet an in his short white bathrobe. There was a book propped up on a shelf in the kitchen. I knew this capur of old. He'd have a glass a wine stationed at his easel an one in the bathroom, one near the book an a couple more placed around the kitchen. Like he'd have one near the sink an one near the cookur an that's the way he worked. He'd take a sip rathur than bring it around the house with him – wine all ovur the house so he could move around an sip – twas an absolute fascination to watch kinda thing. On his bad days twould be whiskey though. Today twas wine.

"Help yourself, darlings," says he.

We watched him. He looked nice in the bathrobe – nice an lean.

"I trust you're cooking for at least three?" Dec.

"I am indeed and always do." He took a swig outa his wine. "Right," said he. "Today we'll be kind to Declan – we'll play some opera."

So we had *Madame Butturfly* an all that stuff an Dec cried in his wine. Till Liam got cantankerous an started up an argument.

"What're we listenin to all that ould Italian for? Couldn't they sing in English?"

"Absolutely not," said Mothur. "English is far too brittle a language – it doesn't *flow* – all those rasping consonants.

Opera *demands* Italian – "

"Wait a minute now – let me stop yeh right theyur!" Liam was dalkin the air with a knife. "Wasn't it you were readin Shakespare for us there one day – that thing about the birds singin in the cold – "

"Bare ruined choirs where late the sweet birds sang?"

"That thing, yes – an weren't you ravin on about the beauty a the English language – "

"Aaah! Yes! The *brilliant* combination of vowels and consonants in that line – "

"Chalk it down," said Liam. "Chalk it down." With the knife at arm's length. "Brilliant, yeh say! But didn't yeh just say consonants rasp? I mean, make up yur mind – are consonants hot or are they not?"

Mothur did his sighin act, hand to the forehead.

At this point Liam changed horses. He didn't actually give a fuck as long as he could argue about somethin. A real Corkman, if yeh like. "To tell yeh the truth, I prefer *not* to undertand what they're sayin."

Dec an Mothur stared at him.

"I mean tis always a lot a crap. I mean listen to that now!" That beautiful thing that everybody knows, outa Whatsit, was playin. "Like an anjul singin. Yeh don't know *what* she's on about – an that's fine – yeh feel all kinds a grand things. Who wants to know she's sayin 'Papa, let me do a line with his nibs or I'll throw meself in the rivur'? That's the one, isn't it? I mean as far as words go, we misewell have Madonna doin *Papa, don't preach*. If yeh ask me, the only thing worth understandin in opera is Madame Butturfly an that ship – "

"You may have a point, Liam," says Mothur in a strained voice. "Perhaps the words don't matter. Opera *is* all about the *unleashing* of emotion . . . "

"My very words," says Liam.

"Denis concedes," says Dec. "Anothur round to our

reigning champion."

"Concedes, how are yeh," says Liam. "He fuckin loses."

Well, concedin or losin, Mothur gave up an got on with his cookin.

Aftur a while Dec spoke up. "Y'know, this is the real epit – what's the word? Epitsomething?"

"Epitome?"

"The real epitome of the bachelur life," said Dec. "If you were married now you couldn't have this carry-on – I mean the glasses all ovur the place and *your* music and *your* choice a wine – to say nothing a Liam and me."

"Married?" The eyebrow went up. "What *are* you thinking of, dahling?"

"I'm thinking about Mike. I mean you want to give up all this – for him."

Mothur had his back to us washin some lettuce. He had just taken the lettuce out of the sink an his hands were very still on it. But he didn't turn round.

"Is that sauce startin to burn?" asked Liam.

Mothur stirred the sauce an turned the heat down.

"You can do it in Denmark y'know," said Liam suddenly.

"Do what, dearest?" asked Mothur.

"Get married. To a fella, like."

"There y'are," said Dec, winkin at Liam. "At last you can make an honest woman a Mary. He deserves it, aftur so long as your common-law wife. A couple a plane tickets and off you go."

Mothur gave him a look an sat down again.

"I'm serious. You should set us all an example. Be a trailblazur. Say: David Norris, bate this in two throws!"

Denis didn't look amused. In fact, the life seemed to have gone outa him. He scowled inta his glass. He pulled the opera tape outa the hi-fi, slammed somethin else in an the kitchen filled up with a real swingin blues guitar. Oh, *great*! Gary Moore. Drippin soul. An he a Belfast man. Roddy Doyle was right.

"*I'd* look on it as my bounden duty if I were you," said Dec. "What with AIDS an all an your position as an eldur of the community." Mothur's eyebrow went up an he scowled at Dec. "Well, I mean you're not an *ancient* exactly but we all look to you for example. Anyway, I don't know how you can resist the idea – you know: to boldly go where no Corkman has evur gone before . . . "

"No Sexually-ambivalent Cork Person, please," said Denis with a bit of a smile. "We must be politically correct whatever."

"We'd make *The Cork Examinur*," said Liam. "Front page."

"Oh, the Ultimate Temptation!" says Mothur.

"What more do you want?" says Liam. "The Late Late Show?"

Gary Moore was handin his soul up on a plate at this stage. The guitar would break your heart.

"I want Mike," said Mothur, all doom an gloom.

"Well, ask *him* so," said Liam with a grin at Dec.

"Ask him what?" says Mothur.

"To marry you," says Dec.

"Alas, my children, he doesn't want me . . . or anyone else." I coulda told him that wasn't true, rememberin Bewley's. He shoulda remembured himself. Talk about demoralised.

"It's just a 'phrase'," said Dec.

"Oh, that *bloody* Michael Jackson!" cried Mothur to the ceilin, liftin his two fists above his head. "I could *cheerfully* break his *neck*!"

"Oh, blame him, do," said Dec. "If it weren't for him you'd have lured Mike into your bed ages ago. Think of it: Mary and Mike, fore and aft, with your bottle a whiskey in one fist and your fags in the othur."

Mothur looked sick. "I know, I know. There's Mary. But I'm lonely and I get so depressed. And maddened by the fact that I can't even argue a case. Jackson is *sacrosanct*. I tried to tell him what I read about nose-jobs recently – "

"What was that?" asked Liam, on the verge a laughin.

"Well, that they *interfere* with the reception of sexual signals but I didn't *dare* to make my point!"

"Which was?"

"Well, that the *problem* with Jackson is not that he's *sexless* but that after all those nose-jobs he is no longer able to sexually differentiate between a *Boy Scout* and a *dolphin* . . . "

Boy Scouts? Dolphins? What the fuck? The mind boggled.

I had to laugh.

I wanted to say to Mothur: Yeah, why couldn't he have fallen for a nice *normal* boy like *Prince*?

None of em said anythin for a while an then Liam spoke up. "Don't miss the bus, Denis, don't miss the bus."

"What he's trying to say is: carpe diem," said Dec.

"C'man, boy," said Liam. "Now's yur chance. *Heal the World* has had its run. He's just released *Give in to me*."

Mothur looked at Liam an hope dawned in his eye. Twas pathetic. "Liam," says he, all heart-felt. "You wouldn't be having me on?"

"Course not," said Liam. "Shur, yeh saw it yurself at the end a the Oprah Winfrey interview. With Slash on guitar. Real steamy."

"Oh yes, oh yes," says Mothur, all breathless. Then: "Is it *Give* in *to me* or *Give* it *to me*?"

"Six a one an a half-dozen a the othur," said Liam.

Mothur sucked in a deep breath. Then he threw back his glass a wine an stared ahead a him, lookin like a man a purpose.

"Captain Picard?" says Dec. "Forgive me now for

draggin yeh back from the frontiers of space and time – but that spaghetti'll be mush . . . "

"*Damn!*" shouted Mothur.

He leapt at the spaghetti.

But now he was on a high. An when Denis is on a high he starts to trot out his hobby-horses.

"Do you realise that Shakespeare spent his *life* surrounded by *transvestites? Minors*, at that."

They did realise. He'd told em before.

"Cleopatra! Juliet! Viola! They were all boys! And the Sonnets! The critics will hardly entertain the notion that the recipient of the Sonnets was an actor – something so likely it is inevitable. Shakespearean scholarship has been *bending over backwards* to prove he was a nobleman. So that they can explain them in terms of *patronage* rather than passion! It doesn't seem to bother them that they thereby rob them of all *meaning.*"

At dinnur twas nothin but Alexandur the Great. We'd heard it all before like. He was always at it. He was real bad about it. All about Alexandur an Hephwhatsisname an their great love an all that. If it wasn't that it would be about Alexandur's Persian boy who was a eunuch, would yeh believe, but that was only when Mothur was half-ossified an fierce maudlin because he useta always weep inta his whiskey he had such a thing about this Persian boy. Oh, he had a major problem about Alexandur the Great, had Mothur. Sometimes twould be the Emperor Hadrian for a change. He had a boy too that he deified an all. If yeh deified someone you were grand in Mothur's book. Twasn't enough to be doin a line with em like – yeh had to wait till they died an deify em. Like Alexandur did with Hephwhatsit. I mean if somebody had thought a deifying *me* Mothur woulda given him an Oscur or a Laurel Wreath or somethin.

"And when they reached the tomb of Patroclus they

anointed themselves in oil and raced naked around it in celebration of that heroic friendship," says Mothur.

The lads' faces were a picture, between amazement an amusement. I can still see em, with their mouths open an the forks full a spaghetti raised to em.

"I didn't know you were into that kinda thing!" Dec.

"Shur I'd be game to try that with yeh any day!" Liam.

"Oh Gawd," cried Mothur to the ceilin. "They have no souls!"

"Don't be personal," said Dec.

"What d'yeh mean?" Liam wanted to know. "Shur didn't we go to Greece with yeh last year an look at all the statchiz? If yeh'd told me that yeh wanted to race round em anointed in oil shur I'da done it with yeh flyin."

Mothur didn't answur. He picked up a cork from the table an started fiddlin with it an he looked so down in the mouth that me two boyos shut up an just watched him ovur their forks a spaghetti. Aftur a fair while he let a huge sigh outa him.

"Oh, what a fall from grace!" says he quietly from his heart.

"What's he on about now?" says Dec. "Bishop Casey?"

I knew what he was on about.

When he sat there broodin for anothur while I saw the lads makin eyes at one anothur. We were always a bit scared a him when he was on this kinda downur. So twas a relief to me when Dec spoke up.

"Red roses," says he.

"What?" said Mothur.

"On the table. An perhaps *La Bohème* . . . " His voice had gone all soft an he was gazin inta space.

"*What* are you talking about?" asked Mothur.

"The proposal," said Dec, as if surprised.

"A ring," said Liam. "Yeh gotta have a ring. That's how it goes, isn't it?"

Mothur crossed his arms an stared at em from undur his brows.

They stared back.

They all stared for a fair while.

"Denis," said Dec at last. "It's about the only thing that might work."

"Sweep him off his feet," said Liam. "I mean with Mike yeh'll really havta grease his butt if yeh want to slide in – uh, I mean – " He shut up. Mothur an Dec were both glarin at him, for different reasons.

But twas lucky he said that as it turned out because Mothur was so offended that he brooded till he got his Captain Picard look back on again. "Are you sure about this Denmark information?" says he at long last.

"Not exactly," said Liam. "But yeh wouldn't wanta find out that it isn't true, would yeh?" Big eyebrow raise.

Mothur's eyes widened. He got the point. He could see himself an Mike in some little hotel in Copenhagen – a room with a view an all that.

"An if yeh ask me," said Liam. "I think he'll go for any chance to get yeh to himself without Mad Mary latched onta yur groin like a fuckin ferret!"

Mothur let a big scairt a laughtur outa him.

"Always the colourful phrase, Liam," said Dec. Very dry. "You should go into advertising. Did yeh evur try those consumur competitions?"

Mothur stood up an did a kinda Picard straightenin a the back before he started clearin the table. There was a glint in his eye an a little smile on his mouth.

The langur might get sense yet.

When we left Mothur's – Dec still in his drag – I was prayin we'd go straight home. But no. The lads had works a mercy on their minds. I had bed on mine.

They wanted to go down to the Simon house – y'know, the home for the homeless an all that. Fuck. The place always gave me the creeps. But now, on top a that, I was scared shitless – what if some ould fella snatched the bag? Jesus! A fate worse than death!

I was just goin to start inta a decade a the Rosary when I thought I'd have a go at some a Mothur's Greek gods for a change. I couldn't remembur any a their names but then Eros popped inta me brain on accounta Eros Ramazzotti on MTV so I tried him. An, fair fucks to him, he came through. Liam decided twould be bettur to go anothur night because he'd bought some fags on the boat for the ould codgers an he'd havta go back home for em. So they called it a day.

I couldn't believe me luck. The relief. I'd thought we'd be spendin the night in that kip – we'd often done it. Like if there was any kinda emergency (like someone dyin – they were at that all the time), we'da been there the night long.

So, soon, very soon, we were climbin Summurhill with me heart poundin – *I wanta be your sledgehammur* – an then we were home an he took me outa the bag an put me on the bedside table with the rosaries an all that. An he lit his candle next to me instead a puttin on the light.

Then he stripped off in a hurry an hid his nun gear an put his cassette playur on the floor next to the bed an threw himself into the bed on his stomach. He pressed the play-button an very very low there was my Vangelis song again an I knew he was thinkin a me:

One world we all come from
One world we melt into one
Just hold my hand and we're there
Somehow we're goin somewhere . . .

The song came to an end an he didn't move.

A cold cold feelin came ovur me.

"*Dec!* Dec boy! Yeh're not leavin me out here in the cold, are yeh? Tis freezin!"

Nothin.

"Dec! Have a heart! I'm cold. Jesus, I'll be cold enough soon enough. Ah, Dec boy! Don't do this to me! Take me in there with yeh, won't yeh?"

Nothin. He was asleep.

Maybe that was the trainin for bein a spirit – the long hours a meditation I suppose yeh'd call it. I mean when I was in the flesh I'd nevur spend hours *thinkin*. If I had nothin to do I'd pick up a book or Q magazine or listen to music or find someone to have a bit of a laugh with or have a pint.

I had all sort a bittur feelins to cope with that night. Honest to God. I was in despair. The grave ahead an partin from him – an them all. An the nasty memory a Taxi Drivur. An bein jealous a Big Dick – an Liz. An worryin about Liam. An Mike an Mothur. An me real mothur. An even rememberin me own death an the pain I'd been through. I brooded an brooded an brooded but in the end I worked meself into a state a trance or somethin an managed to rise above it all so to speak. Well, almost – except for a kinda anxious feelin about them all an a kinda dread at what lay ahead.

So I got one hell of a shock when I felt his hand on me an he lifted me into the bed with him.

He kept his hand on me for a while an then it dropped away an I think he drifted back to sleep. I lay there against his chest an me heart quieted an twas different from the last time. I could feel or I imagined I could feel everythin. I didn't feel as if I was havin a bath with me socks on any more. I could feel his skin. I could feel so well I could count the hairs on his chest.

I lay there in bliss, listenin to his heart an thankin God for being so good to me.

Twas a grand bed. Coulda been designed for me. I was rolled up close against him, almost undur him.

I was waitin for it an it came: the beautiful blissful peace drifted away an I began to feel that ache again, all ovur the body I didn't have. I wanted to move, to stroke, to rub myself all along the muscles of his back an arms – to do what any stray *cat* could do an I couldn't. But it struck me that this was great, that this was like bein *alive*, that being alive was all about movin an wantin an doin. An as long as I was still reachin out I was still alive. I'd have plenty time for peace latur.

He shifted an I rolled down past his ribs an onta his belly. I nearly suffocated with excitement.

Now I was almost where I wanted to be. A push an a shove an I'd be there. I began to sweat. I tried, tried, tried to go down, down, down. With all my will. Rock an roll. The more I rocked an rolled the more I throbbed. I was thrustin with my whole bein an prayin please, God, just this once an then a few scaldin pulsin sensations gripped me like a hand – as if I was comin in short spurts. No! Not yet! *No. No.* This might be the last an only time.

This was a bit too much like pain. Take it easy. Take it easy. Nice an easy. I dragged my breath in an out like as if it were a fishin-net. Like a fishin-net ovur the pebbles a the sea. An the pebbles rollin with the waves. In an out. The water was swirlin.

Easy. Nice an easy.

Prince came to me rescue with a slow slow heavy pulse that filled my head. Like the Mothur a Good Counsel, Prince nevur let me down.

Do me, baby, like you nevur done before . . .

He moved an I rolled an it came up to meet me. Miracle to God, stiff and hard. *Yes!*

I felt I was movin. I felt the silky skin of his dick was movin with me. Or was it he was movin? No – he was asleep, wasn't he?

I was movin with Prince – slow slow heavy an slow. I

no longur knew what was really happenin an what was happenin in my head. The mouth I didn't have closed around the head of his dick – an began to suck hard an easy. I wanted him to be awake! Wake up, love –

Don't want to do it all alone –

and his hands came down on me as if he was holdin my head.

Isn't it supposed to take a long time?

I'm not goin to stop until the war is ovur . . .

His dick was swellin in my mouth an suddenly he gave a few jerks an I hadta bar it with me tongue (what tongue?) an I was just preparin meself to swallow (*how?*) when he calmed down again an I went back into me rhythm. Yeah, love, I had to *die* to become a good lovur. If you were a man a substance you'd be offerin me Harley Davidsons an leadin roles on Broadway if only I don't stop.

It was no time for crackin jokes. Serve me right – I lost me grip. I rolled down the length a his penis to the base an he turned at the same moment an I was pressed hard against the curly hair of his groin. An while I was still shudderin with the delight a that I felt his balls become hard an tight an I knew he was goin to come. Then he turned right ovur on his stomach, felt the hardness of the urun under him an shoved it away an when he came I was lyin helplessly against his hip.

If I had me wits about me I could have got off grand on that but it was such a shock to be shoved away – I felt so *rejected* – I felt like ashes in an urun. I lay there shakin an swallowin an tryin not to cry. An while I was still like that I suddenly rolled an fell outa the bed. I musta been shoved – there was no way yeh could fall outa that bed without being pushed. I dunno if twas deliberate or what – but yeh, he shoved me outa the bed.

I landed with a thump that jarred me to me soul. An I lay there like a fuckin turtle or tortoise or beetle on its back. I'd never been so humiliated in all me life.

The humiliation of not bein able to get up even – of just lyin there like an eejit.

An lie there I did on the cold lino till he woke up late next mornin. I meditated – the propur thing for a spirit to do. What else could I do? So I'd forgiven him by the time he woke up. The first thing he did was he dived for me an put me carefully back on the table with a kinda caress. It hardly made up for bein kicked outa the bed.

CHAPTER 5

THAT NIGHT WAS OSCUR NIGHT AN WITH THE BLOODY THING on at three o'clock in the mornin no chance for me to fall outa any beds at all – unless I was very very lucky. We were all goin to watch the Oscurs at Mothur's an what's more, there was a plan afoot to present Tizzy (Vivien Leigh like) with an Oscur that Mothur had brought back from the States.

But that mornin Dec got inta his drag again – oh, Jesus, what now – an we vamped out to Douglas to see Uncle Ned, Liz's fathur. Normally Dec went there of a Monday night hail rain or shine to mind Uncle Ned an let Liz's mothur go out for the night. But a course he'd missed Monday night that week.

When we got there an rang the bell the door opened an I got one helluva shock. Aunty Kitty, Uncle Ned's sistur, stood there an she encased in this big plastur-cast from hur hips up to hur neck. Hur head was kinda forced back so she was lookin up at us – she's a tiny scrap of a woman. With wavy white hair, bright blue eyes an a narra nose.

"Good morning," says Dec. Real mellow. "I'm collecting for the Vincent de Paul."

"Good morning, Sister," says she, very polite. "Lovely day, isn't it?" She has a high strong Cork voice, a bit genteel, with a lot a life in it, a bit like Dec's own.

Anyway, laugh! She swivelled round like a top in hur cast an went an got hur purse an gave Dec 50p.

He looked at it. "That's not nearly enough," says he. "We don't accept anything less than a pound."

Hur mouth dropped open. Well, it tried to but it couldn't make much of a job of it against the rim a the cast. "But that's what I always give, Sister! I couldn't manage a pound! I only have my penshun!"

"New regulations," said Dec.

She was mouthin like a fish. But at this point it began to dawn on hur. She started to kinda laugh to hurself but she still didn't say anythin. She wasn't sure.

"That cast must be very itchy," says Dec. "Would you like me to scratch your back for you?"

Now she really started to laugh. "Dec! Well, you're a hard case! Well, honest to God!" She was laughin so hard hur eyes were swimmin with tears.

Next thing out comes Uncle Ned, a small little man with silvury-grey hair an the same bright eyes an long nose as Aunty Kitty's. He looked over his glasses, that were way down on his nose, at Dec.

"Hello, Uncle Ned," said Dec.

"Dec?" He was smilin mad. He was aftur gettin his bottom teeth taken out for some reason an that gave him a real sweet cute smile. "Dec, boy, is it you?"

We all went into the sittin-room an sat down in fronta the telly. Uncle Ned spends all his time watchin telly since he had his stroke.

"What's this about, Kit?" Uncle Ned asked Aunty Kitty, kinda nervously hitchin at his trousur-leg in this way he has. He pointed at Dec's gear with this nice strong square hand he has with kinda blunt fingurnails. "What's he dressed like that for?"

"I'm taking the plunge at last, Uncle Ned," said Dec. "I'm entering."

Uncle Ned was gigglin. "D'yeh hear that, Kit?"

"Uncle Ned," said Dec. "Will you give me away?"

"Kit, what's this about?"

"I'm entering the Poor Clares, Uncle Ned," said Dec. "I'm going to be a Bride of Christ and I want to know if you'll give me away?"

"Well, it would be an honour, Dec," said Uncle Ned an he pinched Dec's cheek affectionately as if he was entirely aftur forgettin Dec wasn't a girl. "But you'd want to have a shave first . . . " Big chuckle.

Aunty Kitty was still laughin away, hur eyes all shinin with tears in that way she has – she loves a good laugh. "Well!" says she. "You're a scream, Dec!"

It turned out that Liz was up in bed, the lazy bitch. An her mothur, Aunty Kitty's sistur-in-law – who musta been havin a rare old time if she was takin care a Aunty Kitty in hur cast as well as Liz's fathur – was out. Y'see, the thing is, Uncle Ned won't stay with anyone except Dec or Liz. An he useta give Liz a real hard time tormentin hur about when would Aunty Eileen be back an wasn't she very late an maybe somethin had happened to hur an so on. An sometimes he'd have a real panic-attack. But he loved Dec. Dec knew how to keep him laughin.

Anyway, that day yeh couldn't tell whethur Uncle Ned was really bein fly pretendin to believe Dec or whethur he was confused. The fact he was gigglin most a the time made it hard to know. Y'see, since he had the stroke he's suffured from amnesia a bit an doesn't recognise people sometimes, even people he knows and in general he's aftur gettin very childish. Before, he was a clever kinda man – there was nothin he hadn't read or didn't know about – but aftur the stroke even followin *Star Trek* was too much for him. Though, come to think of it, followin *Star Trek* can be a bit too much for anyone. Anyway, I think that even when he had all his wits about him, before he got sick like, he still wouldn't have seen anythin wrong with Dec wantin to be a nun.

They always had great gas, him an Dec.

That mornin they started up this thing about Aunty Kitty. Like Dec would wait till she was gone outa the room an then he'd nudge Ned. "Who's yer wan?"

An Uncle Ned'd be delighted with this. "I don't know – I was never introduced to her."

"Isn't she the new maid?"

"Is that who she is? I was wondering who she was!"

Aunty Kitty'd come shufflin in an she in the cast.

"Ned, boy, push back from the fire! You'll get chilblains!"

And Dec'd be: "If I were you I wouldn't let her talk to me like that. Don't you ever correct her?"

"Never!"

"*What! Never?*" Singin.

"*Well . . . hardly ever!*"

An this would go on constantly – any time we were there – this "What! *Never?* Well, hardly ever!" outa Gilbert an Sullivan. Othur times I'd been there they'd have records on like *The Mikado* an Dec would sing along with them falsetto. Twould always be light opera with Uncle Ned but what Dec really liked was the real prima donnas. You'd be with him an he'd be playin Maria Callas or Joan Suthurland an he'd be waitin for hur to reach The Note because this was what he loved – the solo singer – an even with the backin of a chorus he'd be waitin for hur to reach The Note – this was the passion he had. He'd go through the record with yeh, tellin yeh the story, the whole lot an how that was the first time she hit that particular note. An in actual fact yeh'd hardly hear anythin an we'd wind it back an wind it back an he'd be "Wait for it! Wait for it!" an I'd be sayin "Great!" but shur how could yeh get it across to him that this was lovely – like I wouldn't be showin enough enthusiasm because *how* could yeh show enough enthusiasm, he was so absorbed by this thing.

Anyway – this day I got pulled out an shown off an put up on the table where I could see the telly. Uncle Ned cried a bit an got invited to the funeral, him an the family like.

I think Dec wanted to cheer Uncle Ned up then so he got him goin about *The Return of the Jedi* that was on Sky an the thing was ruined for anyone who was takin it seriously. Which luckily we weren't. Like when this robot came rattlin down this corridor, rattlin along. Dec started off. "Jesus, he's very bad since the operation!" An like always in Uncle Ned's he kept up a runnin commentary all the way through. Twould drive yeh up the walls. "The plastic surgeon didn't do very well – Jesus, I'd nevur have paid money for that job!" An Uncle Ned chucklin away like mad.

Uncle Ned got back to the enterin again. "I'd a thought you'd a gone for the Butterfly nuns, Dec."

"Aren't those head-dresses just fabulous? Though you wouldn't want to wear em in a high wind – you might take off like!"

"But aren't they the crowd you like? Going into prisons an hospitals an all that? Isn't that what you like?"

"Yes, I admire them. But I've decided the contemplative life is the thing for me – the powur-house of prayur, y'know. The active life and the contemplative – they're complementary, Uncle Ned. C'mere, you won't forget me when I'm in there, will yeh? You know the system: they're totally dependent on the public for food an everything."

"Of course we won't forget you, Dec boy," said Uncle Ned. "Will we, Kit?" Grinnin away. An he patted him on the cheek.

"Uncle Ned," said Dec. "I'm afraid you're not taking this venture seriously. I'm in dead earnest. I mean originally my idea was to beome an anchoress – y'know, to have myself walled up altogethur – but when I enquired about it I discovered that for some reason it's gone out of fashion. Believe it or not, they don't do it any more."

"Ah, Dec boy, we wouldn't let you do that at all!" said Uncle Ned. "Would we, Kit? You mean to be walled up in a little cell for life!"

"Immured is the correct word, Uncle Ned," said Dec.

"No, no, we'd never let yeh do that! Shur that's a terrible life!"

I was comin out in a sweat at the thought of it.

"The fastest way to Heaven, Uncle Ned."

"I'd have me doubts about that now. Shur some of em used to go out of their minds what with the lice an the smell an the dark an the silence – "

"Not at all, Uncle Ned, they became mystics! They'd already left the physical world. Shur where's the darkness when you're illuminated with spiritual light?"

"They still had to go to the toilet, didn't they?"

"Well, yes, I don't deny that – but their minds were on a different plane."

"My mind d'be on a different plane, too, when I'm goin to the toilet."

"Yerra, go way, Uncle Ned! You'd nevur make an anchoress! You'd nevur take it seriously! Shur you'd be laughin – there you'd be in your cell laughin away an they'd think you'd gone off your chuck!"

"C'mere," said Uncle Ned real roguish – gigglin. "Didn't some a them dig their way out with a spoon an it used to take em fourteen years?"

"That was the Count of Monte Cristo, Uncle Ned, and well you know it!"

Uncle Ned was so much inta Dec enterin that when it was time to leave Dec didn't want to spoil the joke by changin back inta his ordinary clothes. So he said goodbye still in his nun gear an we ended up out in the garage with Liz, up outa hur bed by that time, while he changed. Twas chilly an dampish in the garage an it didn't help when he went off on a flight a fancy.

"I have but two hours to live. Come – dress me as for a festival!"

Mary, Queen a fuckin Scots. He had it all off pat. An then he had to throw shapes with his arms outstretched an let Liz undress him an put every stitch a his ordinary clothes on him. "My Lord, I am thankful for the welcome news. You do me great good in withdrawing me from this miserable world out of which I am glad to go, on account of – "

"Did yeh bring any underpants? I can't find any – you must have forgotten em – you'll havta stay in that effort." The black nylon pants Dec was wearin was nevur suitable nun's undurwear – but then how do I know?

"Dress me, my child – my crimson petticoat, my pale blue stockings, my plaid camisole, my kirtle of black satin, my embroidered black gown . . . "

At this stage now Liz was strugglin with his smelly socks an makin a big fuss about it.

"What devotion! I'll remember you in my will, my child – I'll leave you my favourite Skye terrier. Now, bring me my gold-fringed handkerchief, hand me my girdle and cross and put my Agnus Dei about my neck. Thank you, my child – see how happy I am to leave this world!"

Liz was draggin his denim jacket on him.

"This is the last trouble I shall give you – my widow's coif of lawn and lace with the white gauze veil."

Liz wound his big red-an-white scarf around his neck as a finishin touch – twas one a them things like Pakistanis wear.

"Hand me my pomander and rosary. I have finished with the world. Let us kneel and pray together . . . "

"No, no, no!" says she, holdin on to him an stoppin him from kneelin down. "You'll ruin that black satin if you kneel on the filthy floor with it! Get up! Get up!"

An off they went arm in arm. An Liz was carryin me.

It was different bein carried by a woman. A real bumpy ride because the bag kept bangin against hur hip. It felt very awkward. I mean it isn't an efficient way to walk – goin from side to side when yeh're trying to move forward. It must be weird bein a woman, with all those built-in defects, like periods an that. I dunno how God evur left the first woman past the drawin-board stage. I mean twas a real shoddy job. Like he got fed-up halfway through an said "Well, I haven't quite got it right but Jaysis, that'll do."

Dec was talkin. "I mean I hope you know you can nevur marry anyway?"

"Excuse me," says she strongly. "I'm going to marry an have a rake a childrun."

"Well, you know that anyone you want to marry is goin to havta be vetted by me. And there'll be no-one good enough. Niall Ryan certainly isn't – not by a long shot! You'd do bettur to marry me."

I don't havta tell yeh – me heart sank to the bottom a me urun. This was me worst nightmare.

"We'd do our own thing, of course," said Dec.

"Well, thank God for that!" said Liz, laughin.

"It's not that I'm not able for sex with a woman but I get bored with it – I mean halfway through I think 'God, I wish this was ovur!' I keep going like – but – well, it's *alright.* But anyway, twould be incestuous between us."

She laughed again an kinda hugged his arm closur.

"No, I'm serious, Liz!"

"I know you are. And in a way twould be grand, I know. I mean you're the husband everyone wants – and nobody has. I know you'd pampur me to death – cookin an tellin me to take it easy an listenin to all my troubles."

"But you don't understand! That's all nothing! I *love* doing things for you! I mean I *love you*!"

I was dyin. Shrivellin up in me little metal coffin.

"I know," says she. "I know we have a friendship to bate all. But, say we got married, how long would it be before you'd be draggin one a these 'I could have him gutless' types in on top a me?"

"But, Scout's Honour, I wouldn't do that if we were married! I'd have every respect for you. And the childrun – don't forget the childrun!"

She stopped an stared at him. "And what kinda fathur would yeh make, I wondur?"

"I'd make a bettur mothur! I'd make a *great mothur*! You could be the fathur figure. That way they'd have their role models."

I felt like a worm at this stage. An I'd thought Denis was demoralised! Denis was fightin-fit compared to me. There was I thinkin Dec an meself were soul-mates an that he felt some kind of a bond with me, dead an all as I was, when it was clear that if he felt a bond at all twas with Liz. A hard pill to swalla.

More than that. I began to panic. The truth was, I was persuadin meself that the funeral wasn't goin to happen. That somehow he'd hang onta me an I'd be trailin around Cork with him forevur. But if I didn't have a place with him, if I couldn't make him feel I had, there was nothin for me but to be scattured on a cold grave. When I thought of the warmth an comfort a bein close to him, I felt somethin like a knot of tears wellin up in my very soul.

No rest for the wicked. We parted from Liz in town – off to meet the Bonny Boy. An we went down to Loafurs to meet Liam. An I thought we might have a peaceful afturnoon there among the gay courtin couples.

But oh, no. Off with us again. Hot-foot, as they say. Would yeh believe, to find me friend – the one I didn't have – the "Benedictine" who was goin to officiate at me funeral. Remembur I told yeh already that he wasn't really a Benedictine – I'm only callin him that. There are no Benedictines in Cork in fact.

I was in fierce humour aftur the night before an the latest thing with Liz an I had no patience at all with any a this. Twas like me soul was bruised all ovur. If I sound impatient now tis also because I don't want to be tellin yeh about what happened next at all.

"I fancy a monk," said Dec. "Those habits are so cuddly."

So inta one a the churches, where monks are to be found.

I felt like Mission Impossible.

I was lobbed on the floor at Liam's feet an inta the Confessional with Dec. He mustn't have liked the look a the first priest because out he came an inta anothur box. Liam an meself were beginnin to sweat at this stage. Then Liam got jumpy so he got up an went outside. For a fag like. Forgettin me on the floor. Thanks, Liam. Next thing out comes Dec, grabs me up an tears out to Liam. "Success!" says he an off with him.

"Hey!" shouts Liam aftur him. "Where are yeh goin?"

"Into the monastery," says Dec. "I'm goin to discuss it with him. You just hang on there."

Into the monastery. Down a corridor till we arrived at a heavy door. Dec knocked an the door opened. The monk was tall, thin, bit a silvur at the temples but not what yeh'd call middle-aged. Black-rimmed glasses. There was a leathur-covured coach with its back to the door an what happened was that the priest invited Dec to sit there an Dec swung me off his shouldur as he passed around the couch an let me down behind it. Behind. So that's how I didn't see what happened aftur. But I could hear grand. Maybe I shoulda tried to levitate – but I didn't want ta.

I don't want to think about this to say nothin of tellin yeh about it. But in for a penny, in for a pound – misewell be kilt for a sheep as a lamb. No, what I mean is: if I don't tell yeh about this I'll be coppin out, won't I?

Twas kinda weird listenin to em discussin me.

Dec told all or nearly all.

"That's a very sad story you've told me . . . " A silence. "Do you mind if I ask you a question that's a bit personal?"

"Go ahead, Fathur," said Dec.

"Was this Tony your – lover?"

"God, no Fathur! We were friends for years – that's all!" That's all.

"But you cared for him – I can see that."

"To be honest, Fathur, I nevur knew how much I cared until now." He said this quite straight an mattur-a-fact.

"You miss him?"

"Terribly."

"But I suppose you have a friend to – comfort you?"

"I don't, Fathur, no. I don't have anybody." Mattur-a-fact.

A silence.

An then the sound a somethin slidin on the leathur a the sofa. I looked up. The monk had slid his arm along the back a the sofa.

While I watched he let it down. "Well, I'm honoured that you chose to ask me. Why did you pick me?"

"Uh, I thought you looked – uh, sympathetic." It seemed to me that Dec's breath was comin a bit fast.

"Oh, I am! I think it's a tragedy that a young life should be wasted in that way. The problem is promiscuity, isn't it? I believe myself that people should foster caring, lasting relationships . . . " The last bit was smothured an while I was still tryin to deny that what was happenin was happenin the kissin noises started to come through to me. *Jesus Christ! Total horror! This couldn't be happenin to me!* I wished I was dead!

I *was* dead.

I couldn't *believe* I wasn't hearin any protest from Dec. I waited for it – waited for the angry voice or the sound of a kick in the balls or for him to just get up an go! An instead I got nothin but grunts an the sounds a clothes bein hauled about. *Dec! You don't havta do this just to get me scattured!* But, Jesus, he wasn't doin it for me!

One thing I thank God for: twas all ovur *real* fast. So I had to endure the sofa jerkin back an forth for hardly thirty seconds if that. But what nearly left me for dead was the fact I didn't know *what* was goin on! Was he fistin or what? I didn't look like it from what I could see – which was the monastic sandals stickin outa the end a the couch an jerkin about in the air an Dec's feet at the same time appearin an disappearin ovur the back of it. That was the worst part. No. The worst part is that I could hear it all – every grunt an groan an bit a friction. Friction! Without a bit a lube or anythin? Holy God, surely he hadn't produced a tube a KY outa the pocket a his habit? Carryin it around like – you nevur knew when it might come in handy? KY? What about a condom? Dec! What d'yeh think you're doin? I thought I was goin to throw up – but a course that was all in the mind – I mean I couldn't have, not havin anythin to throw up or throw up with. But what did happen is that I kinda blacked out. Everythin went dark before me eyes an I knew no more till we were outside the monastery again in the fresh air.

The first thing I saw was Liam's face starin at Dec an lookin strange. Frownin. "Well?"

"Well, we won't have him," said Dec. "Not if he was the last officiating priest on earth!"

"Why? What's wrong with him?"

Dec's only answur was a sniff. He started to walk quickly away, back down in the Coal Quay direction.

"Hey! Wait up!" Liam was annoyed. "What happened? I thought you said he'd do it!"

For answur Dec opened his mouth an wiggled his tongue from side to side.

"Oh, yeh're not serious!" Liam stood stock still. "Yeh're havin me on!"

Dec walked on.

"Well, tell us what happened so!"

"My child, the least said the bettur. Let us draw a veil of secrecy over the whole sorry affair. You could say twas in the secrecy of the Confessional. By the way, did yeh hear? Cork won by a point."

"Did he give yeh money?"

"Oh, no, no – twas purely for the good of my soul."

Next thing he plunged inta the flowur shop at the cornur a St Augustine Street. Came out with a bunch a carnations an headed for the side door a the church.

"What're yeh doin?"

"Mothur of Good Counsel."

"Yeh can't be *serious*!"

"I am."

"Then yeh're a fuckin hypocrite! Goin in now to pray!"

"No, I'm not!" Dec was angry now. "The hypocrite is back there in the habit! Do you know I haven't been to Holy Communion for two years and do you know how much I want to go? But I can't. I couldn't. So don't call me a hypocrite."

He started to go into the church in a huff but then he turned back. "Look, you've got to come in – group effort, y'know. We need help."

Behind him an ould woman came outa the church, in a headscarf, with jowls on hur. "Declan! How are yeh, boy?" She was loaded down with Dunnes Stores bags an a big black shoppin-bag an a handbag nearly as big again. Anothur neighbour.

"Mrs McCarthy, how are yeh?"

"Shur, I'm grand! Tis a while since we've seen yeh."

"How's himself?"

"Shur, isn't he up in St Finbarr's – they hadta operate last week. They were afraid to touch him at all – they said he'd nevur live through it – he's no stomach at all left by this time. But he's alright, thank God! I've just been in to Hurself about him."

"The best thing you could do," said Dec. "I'm just goin in to Her now with my friend."

"Oh! What're yeh goin in for?" She grabbed Liam's arm an kinda shook it – a bit of a job with all the bags hangin from hur. "Is it exams? Or do yeh have somebody sick belongin to yeh?"

"Eh, no," said Liam.

"Whatevur it is, tis right in yur hand now as soon as yeh ask Hur for it!" An she took Liam's hand an bunched the fingurs a hur right hand inta it – an lost her balance with the weight a the bags an kinda staggured an Liam hadta steady her. "*She nevur let me down yet!* Nevur let me down!" She turned back to Dec. "I'm goin down now to get some net curtains for the back winda although himself says what do we want with nets at the back for? He'd prefer to be able to see out to his ferrets an the dogs. Tis like an izoo at home. Yeh can't see out anyway with all the bird-cages. But I always fancy somebody'd be lookin in at us without nets. The old ones are very yella – "

Liam knew of old that this could go on forevur. "We'd bettur go, Dec . . . "

"If I'd the time I'd come an help yeh choose em," said Dec. "But we have somewhere to go aftur this . . . "

"Ah, shur, I know! You're always very good, Dec boy!"

"I tell yeh what – I'll come up next week an have a look at them and maybe himself will be home by then . . . "

"God willin! Come up for your tea."

"I will, I will!"

Liam took Dec by the arm an hauled him inta the church porch.

"I'll tell himself so, that you'll be comin up."

"Do that, Mrs Mac. Goodbye now!"

A heave from Liam an we were inside facin the shrine. There was Mass on but that didn't stop em kneelin down at the little wooden rail in fronta the shrine. Liam slapped his hands up to his face an pretended to be prayin. Dec threw his bunch a flowurs up onta the altur step. There was anothur few bunches there an a few packets a candles – them night-light ones because there were night-lights all ovur the altur in blue glass covurs. Next thing Dec dragged me outa the bag an propped me up on the rail in fronta him. I looked up at the picture a the Mothur a Good Counsel. I looked at hur an I looked at Dec starin at hur an me angry hurt feelin began to fade away. The minutes went by an a powurful feelin a peace came ovur me. The altur was covured in vases a flowurs. Most of em would be handed in in thanksgivin.

"Liam! Are yeh doin your bit?" muttured Dec at last.

Liam made a face through his fingurs.

"Liam!" Dec hissed.

Liam had a shot at it.

"Don't forget Denis and Mike," muttured Dec aftur a while. "Happy endings are what we want."

Like mine?

I thought I'd bettur have a shot at it meself.

I did me best to focus. I should've been good at it – I was a spirit aftur all. So I focused on the picture an I threw me heart an soul at it. I said the prayur to the Mothur a Good Counsel. It had a kinda rhythm to it: Remembur, O Most Gracious Virgin Mary, that nevur was it known, that anyone who fled to Thy protection . . . Remembur, O Most Gracious Virgin Mary. An then I thought: Let me stay with him an take care a him an if I can't, take care a him for me.

There was a rumblin at our backs. The people were standin up. They started to sing.

O Vergen Modur, lady of Good Counsel,
Sweetest pichure in yur mantle blue,
In all our doubts we fly to dee for guidance,
O Modur, tell me what am I to doo!
OOOOOO Modur, teeell meeeee,
Whaaat am I I I to dooooo!

It was touchin, y'know, when yeh thought a all the troubles bein lifted up to the Mothur with that "Whaaaat am I I I to dooooo!" All the money troubles an the people in hospital an sick children an failed exams an drunkun husbands an battured wives an abused childrun an mental cases an deserted wives an men in prison . . . an sons with AIDS . . . An so much of it always on the shouldurs a the women. I'd say the level a testosterone in the church wouldn't a filled a teaspoon – an most a that from the altur-boys. "She nevur let me down yet." She had hur hands full here in Cork. She'd nevur have the time to take care a the likes a me or a romance between a horny artist an an MJ look-alike, would she? I mean twould hardly have priority like.

They started inta *Faith of Our Fathurs*, a very old-fashioned thing altogethur, not in tune with the spirit a the times at all. This was great gas.

How sweet would be deir childruns' fa-ate,
If dey like dem could die for dee-ee
Fa-ate of our fa-a-du-urs' Holy Fate
We will be trutil-ditil-det!
We will be trutil-ditil-det!

I had to laugh.

Liam was back in good form aftur that. An so was I. So what if Dec was a hoor – I still loved him. An a spirit should be above such things anyway.

"We will be trutilditildet," Liam was still singin while we were walkin down to the Grand Parade. We crossed the road an as luck would have it bumped inta Tizzy comin outa the Capital.

"Regeeena!" shrieked Tizzy. "Shrieked Tizzy": good, eh? I'm gettin good at this, have yeh noticed? Practice makes perfect.

"You're not *crying*!" said Dec. "God, that doesn't say much for Neil Jordan's direction! You mean it doesn't have any effect on yeh the nineteenth time round?"

"Ah no," said Tizzy, dead serious. "I'm not aftur seein it at all. Twas a right bake. I nevur knew – tisn't on in de afturnoons. Dere I was, sittin waitin for it to come on an when it did twas *Lorenzo's Oil*. I didn't know whether to stay dere or to come outa 6 an go inta 8 to see Al Pacino."

"Good grief!" said Dec. "What a dilemma! And how did you solve the problem?"

Like I told yeh before, poor Tizzy didn't evur know when he was bein slagged. "Well, I was more interested in seein Al Pacino dan Susan Sarandon – dough normally I'd have seen dem all by now but I've only been goin to *De Cryin Game* – on accounta why Pacino's up agin Clint an Stephen Rea for Best Actur an normally now I'd be more interested in de women but dis year I care more about Clint an Stephen Rea an I'm scared shitless dey'll give it to Pacino on accounta why dey owe him one, dough dey owe Clint too but dey can give him best Directur or Best Picture an twill be a cryin shame if Stephen Rea doesn't get it but dey'll nevur give it to him up agin dat lot an I tink really Pacino's goin to get it an I'll be suicidal if he does."

Liam an Dec were just standin there starin like they could actually see the words comin outa his mouth. When he stopped they waited. He waited.

"So what did you do?" asked Dec.

"I went in to see Pacino an I tink dey'll – "

"Grand!" said Dec. "Grand! Now we know! Grand!"

"C'man," said Liam. "We're headin ovur to the Co-op."

They started off down the Grand Parade.

"No wondur Bosco fled to Dublin in the half-nine train if Tizzy talked his ear off like that!" said Dec.

"Jaysis, says he, let's make this one a quickie!" said Liam.

"Tell me, Tizzy, were yeh talking about the Oscurs in the bar?" asked Dec.

"Yes," says Tizzy, frownin an bitin his gorgeous lip. "D'yeh tink I put him off?"

"Jesus! Don't tell me you actually *care*! One a those yuppie Dublin faggots!"

"He's from Cork, I tell yeh," said Tizzy, frownin hardur.

"Tizzy's pinin," said Liam.

"I am," said Tizzy. "An what's more I'm nervous about de Oscurs. I mean dey've got to fuckin *win*, y'know?"

"*The Crying Game*?" asked Liam. "Right?"

"Yeah! Jesus, I'll be dyin! I'll be slittin me wrists!"

"But, Scarlett, you're so fickle!" said Dec. "What about your ex?"

"Clint?" said Tizzy, breathless. "I know, shur, I dunno what I want anymore!"

So inta the Quay Co-op with em an up the stairs inta the café.

The café is a lovely old room with wooden floorboards an big tall windas lookin out ovur the rivur – or that branch a the rivur. An they always have a coal fire in this real fancy old fireplace. An people in earrings are always sittin around writin letturs or readin newspapurs an eatin carrot-cake. I always feel very laid-back an mellow in that room.

"I suppose smokin in here would be a major crime?" said Liam. He went ahead an smoked.

Next thing Tizzy blushed an me two boyos started

lookin around to see what caused that. Twas the Co-op guy lobbin coal on the fire.

"Jesus, Tizzy," said Liam. "What d'yeh see in him? He's right scrawny." An Liam a fine one to talk.

"I tink he's lovely," said Tizzy. "Sexy like."

I agreed with Tizzy. The guy was real appealin.

"Nevur seen him at the discos, have you?" said Liam.

"Oh, these are Mothur's crowd really," said Dec, lookin round. "I mean these are the types he should be hanging out with, discussing gay rights and vegetarianism."

"Right fuckin snobs," said Liam. "All workin at bein respectable – bein accepted in the community an all that. They wouldn't be seen dead with us! An political – they're fierce political – shur weren't they all walkin in the Patrick's Day Parade there a few weeks ago."

"Oh God! Wait an I tell ye!" said Tizzy. "D'ye know who I met dis mornin? Laugh!"

"Who?" said Liam, because Tizzy was waitin.

"Fawlty. An he off duty. Goin ovur to de Mercy to visit Cliona. An d'ye know what he was luggin?"

"What?" says Liam.

"A massive pink teddy-bear!" Tizzy showed how big. "For hur!"

Holy Hour.

Cliona had been kept in, a course. I suppose she acted up so much they thought she was dyin.

They started on about Cliona. I didn't want to listen. Didn't particularly want to say a decade a the Rosary eithur. I started lookin out the winda at the rivur. I got to thinkin that nobody in Cork knows how many branches the rivur has an the tourists are baffled outa their minds because yeh keep leavin the rivur an comin upon it again an it keeps comin at yeh from all angles. Most people if yeh asked em couldn't draw a map with the rivur in properly to save their lives. I've heard ould fellas arguin about it in pubs. Then I thought, maybe this kinda vague notion about the rivur comes from the ancient days when Cork was a bog – that's what "Cork" means y'know – a bog. Or maybe tis because they built streets ovur branches a the rivur an nobody has evur sorted out exactly what they done. Like the Coal Quay – tis a street not a quay – but in the old days it was a quay. An yeh can see houses with steps leadin up high to the front door because in the old days they were on canals.

Jaysis, I sound like a fuckin tourist guide.

But anothur thing: the main street, Patrick Street, bends because the rivur it's built on top of bends. I'm laughin to meself now because it's just aftur strikin me – even Patrick Street is bent. Bent double. I tell yeh, there are some very quare things about Cork.

Anyway. Tour ovur.

But then I got to thinkin again: Jaysis, isn't this grand? Who needs a fuckin funeral? I don't an I'm the only dead one around here. Maybe they might forget about it. Maybe they mightn't evur find time to do it. Maybe they might traipse around Cork forevur, meanderin around like the rivur, luggin me with em, an nevur scattur me. An who could ask for anythin more?

Yeah, I'll settle for this, God, this'll do grand. KY Monks an Taxi Drivurs an all.

Shoulda remembured to say that to Mothur a Good Counsel while I was at it. Fuck.

Talk about meanderin, I'm meanderin now – that's a grand word, isn't it? Meandur. I'd bettur get back to me story.

When I came round they were lookin at the LGCN. There was an article on alcoholism that they passed ovur fast. They got stuck in one by a dyke on safe sex – all about sex toys an latex an dams an gloves. Jesus! Like havin an operation!

"Twould make yeh think that maybe you'd prefer a Big Mac," said Dec.

I said to meself I was glad I was dead an didn't havta worry about it all any more. Then I remembured I had othur people to worry about.

"An I tell yeh what – all that stuff's expensive," said Liam. "I mean they talk about safe sex – am I suppose to be buyin all that stuff outa me dole?"

"Cling-film," said Dec.

"Whasdat?" asked Tizzy.

"Cling-flim. I mean that's fun – think a the things you can do with it – I mean apart from smotherin yourself or your partnur. And it's economical. And there's plenty of it – I mean rolls of it."

"But what is it?" asked Tizzy.

"Y'know, the stuff they wrap food in – like if yeh're puttin it in the fridge,"

"*What!* Dat silvur stuff?"

"Not aluminium foil for Chrissake, Tizzy! Holy an Blessed Hour!"

"Tizzy! The stuff like plastic!" said Liam when he had stopped laughin. "Don't ye be usin it for somethin in the hair salon?"

"Oh, yeah! I just calls it plastic."

"Tizzy, you're a scream," said Liam an started leafin through the papur again. "What's this? Your risks compared. Oh, look, d'yeh know what's perfectly safe they say?"

"What?"

"Watchin."

"What!" said Dec. "Are we to be reduced to the level of performing seals? But, c'mere, don't they have any articles on gardening or knitting sweaters? In God's name let's have a look at the Classifieds. We might find '*The answer to everything if we do-o!*'" He took the papur from Liam an opened the ads page. "Right. Look at this: 'Loving heart needs life-long home. If you're genuinely into togetherness then drop a line giving details of my heart's new home.' Aaaaah, isn't that sweet! Dublin. So that's out – he'd have to send his heart down by An Post. 'Dublin gay, honest, loyal and passionate, no wasters please.' Liam, would you classify yerself as a wastur?"

"Give's a look!" Liam tried to take the papur.

"Hould on . . . God, Liam, you didn't tell me you were advertising this month. Listen, Tizzy, listen to Liam's effort: 'Smooth boyish lad with obedient nature seeks bearded dominant guy to worship, adore and love to his dying day.' Great stuff, Liam!"

"Give's a look," said Liam.

"It's all Dublin. Let's have a gandur at the notice-board. There might be something available closur to home like."

So they went an started readin out the ads on the notice-board.

"*Whaat!*" Dec was gapin. He pointed to one a the notices. Liam pushed Tizzy outa the way and stuck his nose up to the ad in question.

Dec read it out. "'Calling Cork. Ten minutes before the train. Can't forget you. Ring at once.' *Tizzy!* It's for you!"

Tizzy was aftur goin white. "Yeer havin me on!" He tried to see but Liam slapped his hand ovur the ad.

"'Tis *Bosco*! He can't forget yeh! Fair dues to yeh, Tizzy!"

"Yeer razzin me, aren't ye? Dere's nothing dere, shur dere isn't?"

Probably wasn't, God forgive em.

"What d'yeh take us for?" asked Liam.

A pair a blackguards.

Tizzy pushed Liam's hand away an his own hands were shakin. He read the ad an his lips were movin while he read it. Then he just stared at it. "Maybe tisn't me!"

So it was there.

"Yeh eejit!" said Liam. "Who else could it be? Ten minutes before the train!"

"D'yeh tink so?"

"Did he give yeh his numbur?"

"Yeah . . . in case I evur was in Dublin like . . . "

"An does he have an address for you?"

"No."

"Well, there yeh are!"

Tizzy couldn't believe his luck. Dotin on this Bosco fella. He went off to the phone all in a tizzy.

Me two boyos sat down again. "Quite a day," said Dec. "I'm tired. Aftur last night."

"Oh, twould be nothin to do with this afturnoon's capur?"

"He did all the work." He lay his head down on the table on his arms. When he spoke his voice was muffled. "Took me back."

"Back to what?"

"Back to the Brothurs . . . "

"Oh? Is that why yeh were drummed out?"

Dec raised his head. "I *wasn't*! I left." He dropped his head again.

"Tell us more."

Dec turned his head to the side. "I stuck it out as long as I could. His name was Petur. He was small. That is, his dick was very small. He was straight. I don't know what he was doing in the Brothurs. Like, y'know . . . anyway, he's left since. And he's married since. I liked him. I liked him very much. We were caught alright one day. By anothur priest. He knew damn well what we were doing. There was a knock on my door. Fathur Tom. I was blushing. And I mean the aroma of – y'know – lust in the air. And Petur just sat there grinning. No conscience. From what he told me there were women as well. Up the mountains. I thought Fathur Tom would freak but he didn't. But he went and told the Superiur and the Superiur called Petur to his office and blew him out. 'How could you play around with a soul like that!' And didn't he tell the Superiur everything I'd told him. About my past and my life. And I'd told him the lot – one night aftur he got me drunk. When I was told what he'd said I was very angry. I got in a tempur. I wasn't being thrown out or anything like that. But I couldn't look at him at Mass without my stomach turning. The *piousity* of him! These perfect genuflections aftur what he'd done to me! I didn't storm out the day he reported. I waited. I stopped going to Mass. I wanted to kill him. I wanted to see him suffur. I really did. I suppose I knew it was just a mattur of time before I left. I was consumed with angur and I couldn't forgive him so I couldn't go to Holy Communion. There was no way I could go to Confession with him an his piousity in fronta my face all the time. I didn't want to leave. I mean I wanted to be a Brothur always. Then what really put the kibosh on it, the Superiur sent me for therapy! I didn't see *him* bein sent for therapy! And they started asking me crap about did I want to sleep with my mothur! I mean, I ask yeh! In the end I just felt so unhappy I left."

Liam said nothin, just smoked away an Dec kept his head down.

"Twas him alright!" Tizzy was back with his face all lit up an claspin his hands togethur like he does. "Twas him! He's comin down! He's comin down!"

"She's a-comin, Mistah Butlah – I don't know why she-s comin but she-s a-comin!" said Dec, sittin up.

"He's comin! I can't believe it! First he wanted me to go up but I told him about de funeral so he said he'd come down!"

"Will yeh sit down, boy!" said Liam.

Tizzy sat down. His eyes were shinin. "He phoned as soon as he got off de train an he got it put up."

"So 'I can't forget yeh' means 'I was thinkin a yeh on an off for the three hours it took the train to get to Dublin'," said Liam. "There's somethin seriously wrong with this guy's notion a time. It must come from directin filums – y'know – two minute takes an all that."

"Listen, if he tells you he'll love yeh forevur I'd question him very closely on that," said Dec.

"But, still an all, fair dues to yeh, Tizzy!" said Liam, shakin his head like an ould fella in a pub. "Yeh must have an A1 ass there! The man is actin as if he's aftur strikin gold! C'mere, what kind of a type is he anyway?"

"He's big an blond an in his thirties maybe an he listens a lot – "

"Oh, he's ideal for yeh so!" said Liam, laughin. "Yeh've found someone who'll listen to yeh – well!"

An I had a sudden flash a Tizzy in the Met holdin forth about the Oscurs an yur man from Dublin listenin, maybe real amused an at the same time lustin aftur that gorgeous mouth . . . But maybe twasn't like that at all – maybe he just couldn't wait to check out the one ball?

"So now the question is whethur it was your conversation or your ass enflamed him?" said Dec. "What's your own opinion?"

"He said – he said – " Tizzy blushed.

"Spare us the details," said Dec. "Or you could tell us ovur a drink . . . "

"C'man an I'll buy ye one in de Phoenix!" said Tizzy.

"Ah, we couldn't!" said Dec an Liam together, leppin to their feet an draggin him off before he could even drink his coffee.

CHAPTER 6

So: Oscur night. An the grave approachin at a mile a minute.

We walked inta the club an Dec planked me up on the table.

"Mind that – tis me brothur," says Liam.

I looked around an I thought I was hallucinatin. There was someone up on the stage dressed up as a Guard – the very *head* off Lethil Weapon – an he singin away. An of all things in the worlds, he was singin *The Travellin People*. Just then fuckit, someone put a pint glass, half-full a orange, down in fronta me an I hadta watch through two thicknesses a dirty glass. Like an arty video.

Then I noticed Fawlty sittin to me right. What was he doin there? It dawned on me then that the fuckur on the stage really was Lethil. How in God's name had they got him up there?

I'm a freeborn man of the travellin people
Got no fixed abode, with nomads I am numbured . . .

Well, honest to God! Yeh don't know anybody till yeh get em to sing a song. Was this how the man saw himself? The whole place was in stitches. Twas amazin he didn't see the joke himself. I mean the man spends his time makin grief for travellurs mad enough to park their caravans in his area. But he sang away regardless – grand

133

voice that he has –

Then we'd pack our load and be on the road
Those were good old times for a rovur . . .

He got a terrific round a applause with ferocious foot-stampin from the chickuns. An down he came, dead pleased with himself, with Mothur welcomin him like a long-lost brothur.

"Well done, my *dear* Sergeant! Do sit down! Let me give you a drink. Orange-juice only, I'm afraid!"

Talk about Sleepin with the Enemy.

Lethil could hardly say no when Mothur pressed the drink inta his hand. He sat down an took a swalla an a quare look passed ovur his face. Oh God, what the fuck was Mothur up to? I could stake me life on it that the orange was laced with vodka. Lethil took anothur sip. I took a sconce at Fawlty an he was watchin Lethil outa the cornur of his eye. Lethil said nothin so Fawlty relaxed an took a big slug outa his drink too.

"Dowtcha, Sergeant, that was mega," said Liam. "You've a noble call now!"

Lethil looked around. Mike in his hat was fair game. "Alrright – I call on Michael Jackson overr therre."

So up went Mike an started settin up his backin-tapes an all that an the next thing Cliona came bouncin up to us, dressed in a school uniform – very short. She dragged Fawlty onta one a the benches an clung hurself up agin him. "Was I good?" In a little girl voice, flashin him a big stretch a thigh in the short gym-slip at the same time. She still had goose-pimples. She musta done some kinda act before we arrived – thanks be to God I missed it.

But Fawlty was distracted before he could answur.

"How are yeh, Faawlty?" There was Mad Mary with big silvur earrings danglin, in denim shorts an black stockins an suspendurs. She clung hurself up agin him on the othur side an ran hur hand up his thigh.

The poor man was mortified. "I missed you at the hospital," says he to Cliona. "*Uh!*"

The *Uh!* was because Mary was aftur doin the thigh-run thing again – a home run this time. Mary smiled across at Cliona.

"Mary isn't lookin her usual hideous self," said Dec. "Quite stylish I must say."

"You exaggerate, Declan," said Mothur. "I hardly think the boundaries of style are yet in sight."

Mary looked doubtful. He didn't know whethur that was a compliment or not. So he shrugged his bony shouldurs an moved on to openin an closin the breast-pockets a the Law.

Dec was lookin stylish himself. In a check shirt with a big leathur belt an red scarf round his neck. Denis remarked he looked the head off Jeanette MacDonald – y'know, Golden Girl a the West or whatevur. All he needed was the split skirt – eh, sorry, divided skirt I mean.

Suddenly Mothur stiffened like a dog pointin. Mike was on, doin his professional Jackson stuff. Did I tell yeh? That he's won competitions in England an all for it? What brought him back trailin around Cork I don't know – he coulda made a livin from it ovur. This time he was singin *Don't Stop 'til You Get Enough* – y'know the one, that clinketty-clanketty thing with all the big bubbles in the video. With the two voices, this sexy falsetto an his ordinary voice – so it sounds like he's sufferin from severe schizophrenia?

This was always agony for Mothur. There he'd be clutchin various bits a his anatomy an tearin his hair. The hand splayed out across the heart was a favourite one. At least I didn't havta watch pelvic thrusts from Dec – sittin there sedately with his legs crossed an his back straight.

I'm melting like I can't go on sang Mike.

"Oh Gawd! I've got to have him or die!" Denis, throwin

back a glass a neat vodka.

"Control yourself," says Dec, very severe. "That kinda thing won't get yeh anywhere."

"My God, I'll be driven to rape!" Completely forgettin the presence a the Law.

Lethil did his best to look polite an pleasant an interested in a mild kinda way. Y'know, a polite little smile on his face.

Fawlty wasn't listenin. Cliona was whisperin in his ear an Mary was lookin dangerous. As if she might move on to his fly. He musta been feelin the heat because at this point he took off his jacket an loosened his tie.

"Cockteasur," said Dec. Meanin Mike.

Mothur's face said he was willin to have his cock teased any time a the day or night. "This boy is going to be the *death* of me! Oh, my heart and my soul!"

"Is that where you're feelin it?" asked Liam.

Keep on comin

Til you get enough . . .

Poor Mothur. I pitied him.

I pitied him. An I envied him. God, if I was him! To be there in the flesh! To be able to Go for It!

An goin for it he was. When Mike came down he pulled him down next to him on the bench an put an arm around him. Mike blushed for once in his life an maybe to covur his confusion reached out to me. Mothur smiled an put his hand on the back a Mike's neck, undur his hair. An I could feel the tremble come right down through the fingurs that were just touchin the urun. Oh, man! says I to Denis, yeh're doin somethin right tonight! An suddenly I was stuck in their groove an everythin shifted, like slow motion in a filum, an I could feel the damp thick hair through Mothur's fingurs an at the same time feel the weight an warmth a Mothur's arm across Mike's back. Weird – an *man* was I gettin aroused! How had Mike held out so long against this? Did the mothurfuckur function at all like? In othur words, could he get it up?

Mothur stood up to pour more "orange" an Mike moved his hand away an I tell yeh, I felt faint. Mind yeh, what didn't help was bein choked up with all that cigarette smoke. Worse again, sometimes someone would be aimin at the ashtray or think I was it an I'd get this showur a ash down on topa me. God, twas gross! An I useta smoke! Jesus, I'm cured now. An if you're a smokur yerself, in God's Holy Name give it up. Maybe twas because I was ashes meself that I had such a change a heart – I mean like a cow might feel about a feed a beef stew – but no, tis a disgustin habit without a doubt.

Fawlty, me brave bucko, who was *definitely* off duty an who'd nevur had it so good, was takin a lot a no notice of his superiur's presence. An who'd blame him? Now that he was in his shirt-sleeves Cliona was rubbin hur tits up an down his arm – she had a definite advantage ovur Mary in that department. But Mary was like a mole workin undurground, not a word outa him.

Someone touched me. Twas Mike again. He was sittin there smilin a bit but lookin thoughtful. He started strokin the urun with his first fingur an – I was gettin good at this – I felt this kinda waitin feelin from him, like somebody who thinks he's heard a noise like a knock on the door an is waitin to hear it again.

"Sergeant," said Dec, leanin across to Lethil. "Your rendering of *Travelling People* was superb. But why not *A Nation Once Again*?"

"Politics are no longer fashionable, Declan," said Mothur.

"Tis all very fine," said Dec. "Tis all very fine an fashionable an what-have-you not to be political, but no offence, now, Denis, you bein a Protestant an I know ye're human an all that but I mean – aftur all ye done to us! Are we supposed to forget all our forefathurs suffured now? I mean, weren't they up at our door the othur day – fundraising – Home for the Protestant Eldurly! I mean shur what homes had we? Ye took all we had from us!"

Mothur was well up to him. "Darling," said he. "I know you left school at fourteen and were taught history by your Aunty Aggie who was in Cumann na mBan and got herself arrested and I forgive you your garbled version on those grounds – but *shut the fuck up*, will you?"

Jesus, but Dec could be chronic when he started on this Kevin Barry stuff. Twas one thing I didn't like at all. Mind yeh, he had a point – I mean a few years ago we were all singin *The Men behind the Wiyur* an now we're all Healin the World an eatin those tuna that are friendly to dolphins.

But myself, I call that progress.

At this point Lethil called here to himself an blew the whistle on his fraternisin with the natives, so he and Fawlty headed off. An soon aftur our lot got themselves togethur to go on to Mothur's place for the Oscurs.

"So your beau went off and left you?" said Mothur to Cliona, very bitchy for him, when we were goin down the stairs.

"Oh, he'll be ovur at the station," said Cliona. "I'll call in – he told me he's off duty now."

Which made it very funny when we hit the street an saw the Squad car flashin past us with Fawlty at the wheel an Mad Mary in the passenjur-seat.

Everyone except Cliona burst out laughin.

"Oh dear," said Mothur. "Is he in for a surprise!" He put an arm around Mike an kinda hugged him.

Cliona's face was a picture. She was just kinda mouthin – an that bitch is nevur at a loss. I enjoyed that moment, I tell yeh.

"He'll lose anothur Squad car sure as God," said Liz.

"An whatevur happens we'll be blempt!" said Liam.

"Oh, I wouldn't worry," said Dec. "I don't imagine Mary will keep him occupied very long. A Brief Encountur, I'm sure."

"I wouldn't be too sure she can't keep him occupied," said Mothur an then looked as if he coulda bitten his tongue off.

"You should know," said Dec.

Mothur tightened his hold on Mike as if he was afraid he might take off.

"Where's the Bonny Boy tonight, Liz?" asked Dec when we were goin down the street.

"At home being brought up cocoa by his mammy," called out Cliona, kinda nasty, an she burst out singin:

Oh the bonny boy is young but he's growin!
At the age of sixteen years he was a married man
And at the age of seventeen the fathur of a son . . .

Liz looked embarrassed an titillated an annoyed all at the same time. An worried with it.

I was havin a gandur at all a them. Tizzy was on the moon – Bosco was written all ovur his face. He probably saw himself at the Oscurs in Los Angeles next year or maybe in some Dublin penthouse between black silk sheets: "Darling, I have just four minutes and fifty-three seconds before the train by my Collector's Item Swatch Watch – turn over." Or maybe he just imagined himself sittin in Loafurs, with Bosco sayin: "What'll yeh have?"

Mothur looked like someone who had just caught a sparrow in his hands that he didn't want to let go an he didn't want to hurt.

Mike looked like someone havin a very pleasant private conversation with his soul or MJ.

Dec looked like Jeanette MacDonald half on her ear, carryin two bottles a vodka.

Cliona looked insane.

I dunno, but to me – me brothur looked alone.

"Tizzy," called Dec. "Don't forget to lay in a good supply of KY now for the weekend."

Yeh could feel Tizzy's blush through the dark.

"And I'll let yeh have some of my mothur's Buttur Vouchurs from the Dole – it wouldn't do to get caught short."

"What's this about?" came Mothur's voice from in front.

"The RTE Rapist is hittin town again at the weekend," said Liam. "Would yeh believe breakin in our little virgin here was such a powur-trip he's actually goin to lay out the money on anothur CIE ticket. Even at that, he probably can't get a cheapur deal in Dublin. Yeh moron, Tizzy!"

When we got to Mothur's flat they had already started the run-up to the Oscurs on Sky. Poor Tizzy was pitiful to see – or to feel in my case because he threw me inta an awful state a nerves. He was all in a foostur riggin up the video an all that before we were in the door.

"Tizzy, will yeh stop feckin around with that an get dressed," said Liam.

"Dressed?" Tizzy looked at him stupid.

"Yes! Yeh have to be properly dressed to receive yur Oscur."

"Me Oscur?" Tizzy didn't know what was goin on.

Mothur went into the bedroom an came out with the Oscur so they all had a dekko at it.

Next thing Dec took me outa the bag an put me on the coffee-table in fronta the telly. "We misewell let Tony have a grandstand view," says he an that nearly made me cry.

"You'd miss Tony," said Mothur with a sigh.

"Well, I suppose he's here with us," said Dec very mattur-a-fact. There was a small silence where I heard the ter-ump a me heart missin a beat. "Well, where else would he be?" said Dec into the silence. An there I was, tryin to swalla me tears.

Mothur disappeared into the bedroom.

"It nevur struck me before," said Dec. "The Oscar – it's totally *phallic* isn't it?"

"Hand it ovur to me here and I'll give you an expert opinion," said Liam. "God, yeah! With that head on it an all. An just the right size to get a grip on." He hefted it. "Try it for size there, Dec."

"I'm not *into* sado-masochism," says Dec. "The idea of being impaled doesn't do anything for me, oddly enough. But, Tizzy, twill come in fierce handy when you're up in Dublin in the penthouse and Bosco is outa town on a business-trip."

But Tizzy wasn't listenin – he was back in fronta the telly gnawin his fingurnails.

So they passed the Oscur around an gave their verdicts on how phallic it was. Then they put it down next to me. I felt like an Award meself. It didn't strike any of em how phallic I was, in me urun.

Mothur came back out in his tuxedo an bow-tie, lookin good enough to eat. He was really doin his bit for Tizzy.

"We were just saying, Denis, how phallic Oscar is," said Dec.

"Yes," said Mothur. "But singularly inadequate in certain other respects."

"Thrrue forr ou," said Dec. "Oh, Lord, Tizzy and Oscar togethur – that'll be stalemate."

So they carted Tizzy off to do him up. The poor craytur was so paralysed with nerves about his *Unforgiven* an his *Crying Game* he couldn't have been worse if he really was goin for an Oscur himself. Cliona had supplied the gown for Tizzy – a flashy green-blue thing so tight he looked for all the world like a mermaid an had to walk like one. An a course make-up an a long drape thing.

"But – but you're a gauzur, Tizzy!" said Liam, amazed.

There were great jokes about Tizzy suin Versace when Emma Thompson arrived (on screen like) in a scaly green-blue thing just like Tizzy's. But poor Tizzy hardly laughed – there he was with his whole heart an soul hangin out, glued to the screen.

They all settled down at last with peanuts an crisps an enough alcohol to make sure they'd all be paralatic by mornin – this thing was goin on till half-six or somethin.

Jesus, when was anyone to have a sex-life? No-one seemed to be interested except me. Guzzlin vodka an beer seemed to be their idea a craic.

When Mothur stopped foosterin around arrangin things he turned out the lights an came to sit down. Mike slid to the floor an let him sit in the armchair an Mothur very naturally put a hand on his shouldur an Mike very naturally leaned up agin Mothur's leg. But we weren't very far into the show before I noticed Mike had somehow navigated so now he was sittin between Mothur's legs with his head leanin back agin Mothur's thigh an gettin his neck stroked an his hair worked ovur like Mothur was searchin for lice. Nice work if yeh can get it. Mothur was hilarious to watch. He was rivetted to the TV screen – he'd nevur been so interested in anythin in his life before. Concentration! You've no idea! He was so fascinated by these Oscurs he was even forgettin to smoke or drink.

The othurs, except Tizzy, were in fine fettle an got more raucous as time went on. Twas "Who's yur wan with the tits?" an "I could bonk him senseless" all the way through.

They were all agog to get a gandur at Jaye Davidson because nobody knew if he'd be there as a man or a woman. We got our first glimpse a him when the presentur – Billy Whatsit – was doin the medley at the start: *Those eyes – Those thighs – Surprise! – It's the Crying Game!* There he was, neithur flesh nor fowl – in what looked like a kinda unisex suit with his hair pulled back like a girl. Yeh must understand, we could only see the top half a him so the othurs had a fierce squabble about whether twas a dress or a suit an so on. All Tizzy could say was "Isn't he *beautsiful*! Isn't he just *beautsiful*!"

It was a weird Oscurs altogethur – all the jokes were about Jaye an crossdressin an breakthrough an how women had got a toehold in a category that was traditionally male – Best Supporting Actur. How Jaye was supposed to feel about all that I dunno – I mean he's a guy. An then there was this wan in a white beret who went up an made a speech about deviants – people who aren't accepted because they're not normal or somethin like that – an how was Jaye supposed to feel about *that*? Sittin there in public an bein called a deviant an havin to clap politely? She really sounded a right eejit an it was all so insultin the lads threw popcorn an peanuts at the screen an called hur a stupid cunt an a few choice things like that. Though the poor cow was probably readin a prepared speech God knows.

When the Best Actress came up they put on the lights, turned down the sound, brought Captain Picard back from Outur Space an presented Tizzy with his Oscur while Emma Thompson was gettin hurs.

Mothur presented it. He made a grand speech about Vivien Leigh's *outstandin* contribution to filum and goin on to talk about hur *transcendent* beauty that had illuminated the silvur screen for decades and how hur startlingly *inane femininity* had *entranced* generations a movie-goers. He got loud applause all the way through but when he finished up by sayin that the Oscur was also a consolation prize for the fact that hur husband Laurence Olivier actually wanted to go down on Danny Kaye – well, his audience were in hysterics. The reason I remembur it so well is because Dec remembured it word-perfect an spent the rest a the night repeatin it. I still don't know what "inane" or "transcendent" mean – well, I couldn't dive for Mothur's dictionaries, could I? Like I useta do when I was in the flesh. Or ask Dec – or Liam who was good at crosswords an could surprise yeh at times what he knew in the way a words.

Tizzy wasn't on the high he shoulda been though, gettin his Oscur, because his Jaye had lost Best Supportin Actur to Gene Hackman. "How could they *not* give it to him? How could they *not* give it to him?" The fact that Gene Hackman was winnin for his ex's *Unforgiven* didn't soften the blow much. But Tizzy wasn't the only one upset eithur because we were all backin Neil Jordan like mad an hopin it might be anothur *My Left Foot* night. Twas worse than the Eurovision Song Contest, I swear.

Mike was a bit down in the mouth because MJ hadn't turned up an he'd been expectin him. They all have their little quirks. Whethur to cheer him up or what, when Elizabeth Taylor was gettin her Humanitarian Award for her AIDS campaign, Liam jumped up an grabbed me from the table.

"And to Michael Jackson," says he. "For his personal campaign against AIDS. You're a shinin example to us all, Michael – please accept this Special Humanitarian Award in the form of a pulverised AIDS victim." An while they were all peggin popcorn an peanuts at him, he lobbed the urun at Mike who caught it neatly, thanks be to God an His Blessed Mothur. *That* was a new experience – soarin through the air with the greatest of ease like that darin young man on the flyin trapeze.

When me ashes had settled I tried to get me bearins an for a while I couldn't figure what was wrong. I thought I was feelin faint aftur me trapeze act.

But that wasn't it. What had happened was Mike had kept his hands on me where I was on the floor between his legs. Now I was directly plugged into the Mike-Denis closed circuit an straight off I was out in a sweat. Mothur a course was all ovur him, kissin him on the ear an so on.

This was ferocious – to be stuck in somebody else's charge. The Oscurs were suddenly like at the end of a dark tunnel. I could see the telly but it was very far away an small.

Twas my misfortune then that Tizzy mentioned that Marlene Dietrich once said that when you're dyin they quickly give you an award an the lads got the notion a presentin Jeanette MacDonald (Dec) with a Death-bed Award for Life-time Achievement, so they all rushed into the bedroom to lay Dec out on the bed. That left only Tizzy, glued to the screen. An Mothur an Mike an me.

Tizzy turned off the lights. At once Mothur slid down off his chair onta the floor, got Mike in a grip between his legs, pulled his head back against his left shouldur an started to kiss him long an deep an hard. An when Mothur slid down behind Mike what happened was that Mike was pushed forward against me. So there I was, clung up against Mike's groin. Ho-ly Je-sus.

Now I bet you're thinkin this was a turn-on? You might think this was fun. You might think any sexually deprived spirit like me would be thankin his lucky stars for this kinda opportunity. Group sex is the big fantasy, right?

Wrong. Wrong, wrong, wrong.

It was frightenin. It was fuckin *terrifyin*. I thought: thank God tis just a kiss. I thought: if they go any furthur I'm goin to be really pulverised. I thought: if they go any furthur I'm goin to go out like a light an I'll be extinct forevur. I mean it felt like bein fuckin *electrocuted*. I've thought about it since an I figure it must be somethin genetic in spirits – I mean othurwise we'd spend every wakin moment plugged into somebody's sex-life, wouldn't we? I mean the aftur-life would be a total *orgy*. I'm tellin yeh now – it doesn't work like that.

I was fightin to hang onta me consciousness, y'know?

The rest of em were laughin like hyenas in the othur room – takin photos, makin speeches. Tizzy was chewin his knuckles an starin bug-eyed at the screen. Mothur was givin Mike a tonsillectomy. I was in an urun that was just about to go inta orbit. One thing – I had no furthur doubts about whethur Mike was functionin. He had a fuckin enormous erection an I felt every twitch a the thing, I tell yeh. Unless twas like when yeh think yeh have a gum-boil an when yeh feel it with yur tongue it feels like a bloody great tumour – an then when yeh put yur fingur in yeh find out tis just a tiny pimple aftur all.

I was tryin to gathur me wits enough to sing *Little Red Corvette* or, failin that, say a decade a the Rosary when I was Saved. A hand came down, Denis's, ovur Mike's crotch – an pushed me away, a course.

Twas like the moment when a drownin man is tossed up on the beach by a wave. I lay there gaspin an thankin God for life. When I came round they were still at it but now I was fine. Shaky but fine. An real giggly. Reaction, y'know. I wished Dec was right there so I could dig him in the ribs an crack jokes about it all.

"Denis, you'd really want to get those vicious belts off him – you'll do yourself a severe injury." Dec's lovely crackly voice came outa the dark an everythin was alright again. Denis threw back his head an laughed an twould break yur heart how happy that laugh sounded. He hugged Mike an started feedin him peanuts.

Yeah! Things were really lookin up. Neil Jordan got an Oscur for his screenplay an they all went wild. Tizzy started cryin. Neil Jordan said he nearly missed collectin his award because he was in the bathroom.

"What the fuck were yeh doin in there, Neil?"

"Yeh *dirty* old purvurt! Yeh nobbur yeh!"

"Chasin yur bazz!"

They loved it.

Then disastur struck. Neil forgot to give Jaye a mention.
An Interfuckinnational Incident. Twas absolutely pathetic.
There was Jaye clappin away with a heart an a half an Neil
thanked Stephen Rea an Miranda Richardson an went on to
thank his mothur. There was a kinda silence at the Awards
– yeh could feel the audience waitin for the name, ready to
clap – an it didn't come.

Tizzy stopped cryin. Tizzy looked sick.

"C'mere," said Liam. "Rewind there a second – I want to
see something."

"I can't" said Tizzy. "I'm still recordin."

"Did anybody notice that fella with Jaye Davidson?"

"No – why?"

"I think I know him."

"*Whaaat???*"

"*Rewind! Rewind!*"

"I can't!" says Tizzy in agony. "I'll miss sometin!"

"*Rewind!*"

Liam grabbed the remote control. He rewound.

"*Pause! Pause!*"

Liam paused. The screen started jumpin an no-one
could see anythin.

"I'm missin everytin!" says Tizzy.

The screen steadied up.

"I know him," said Liam. "What's his name – Moore?
He's from Dublin, for Chrissake! He's a hairdressur. But
where was it we useta meet him? Was it Dublin or
London?"

"He does look familiar," said Mothur.

"And does *his* mothur know he's up an down with
hur?" Dec, a course.

"Ah," said Liz. "That's where the flowurs for Mothur's
Day pay off."

Tizzy's night was saved.

"There y'are now, Tizzy! Next year it'll be you!" said

Dec. "Wait till Bosco gets nominated – there you'll be next to him."

"We'll be here next year," said Liz. "And we'll be rewinding an we'll be saying 'Wasn't that Tizzy?!'"

Tizzy could see it all. He was there already.

By the time Clint collected his Awards for Best Directur an Best Filum, Tizzy was prostrate – actually lyin down on the couch in a state a somethin between ecstasy an nervous exhaustion.

By which time it was seven a'clock in the mornin.

By which time they were all fluthured outa their brains but still no-one thought a goin home.

They had just slapped on some music an started dancin when the doorbell rang. "Mary," said Dec an hurried off to the door.

In walks Mad Mary. With this enormous fuckin teddy-bear in his arms. Pink.

"Payment in kind?" asked Dec. Real dry.

"Where did yeh get *that?*" asked Liam.

"He gave iss ta me, didn't he?" said Mary an he was chewin gum in a way that would drive me up the walls if he kept it up.

"Fawlty?" asked Liz, with hur voice high in amazement.

"Who else, gaairl!" An he flopped down on an armchair an started kissin the bear. He looked a fuckin sight with the hair-piece hangin off an his mascara all smudged an a big laddur down his stockin. Propur flahed-out. He started stickin pieces a chewin-gum from his mouth onta the eyes a the bear.

"Dat's de bear he bought for you, Cliona," said Tizzy. "Dat he took to de hospital."

You could see the whites a Cliona's eyes.

"You'll havta give it to Cliona," said Liam. "Tis hurs by right."

"G'waan, baaoy! Fuck aaff!"

"Ah, fair's fair, now, Mary!" said Liam.

"Tis my fuckin bear," said Mary. "Twas me he giyave iss ta! Noss hur!"

"Don't worry," said Cliona, real nasty. "It's the last thing I'd want."

"Yeh weren't with him all night, were yeh Mary?" asked Liam.

"Mind yur own fuckin business!" An he sprawled there, delighted with his bear, draggin at its ears an pullin the gum on an off its eyes.

"Jesus, but you're a hard case," said Liam.

"Is he any good, though?" asked Dec.

"Wouldn't ya like ta know!"

Next thing he got up, bear an all, rooted in his small shouldur-purse an pulled out a cassette tape. He flipped Mothur's cassette outa the hi-fi an slammed in his own.

Madonna, for Chrissake.

Then he sat the bear down carefully on the armchair an looked around.

Liam was in there like a shot, fair fucks to him. Denis had been keepin a very low profile. Scared shitless that Mary was goin to drag him off to bed in fronta Mike. But Liam was the Hero of the Hour. He grabbed Mary an started dancin. With Mary twas a case a second wind. All of a sudden he had great taspy on him, singin along with Madonna soundin like he had a clothes-peg on his nose.

Like a vergin
Touched for de very first time
Like a ve-e-e-ergin!
When yer heart beats nex to mine!

I dunno who sounded worse, Mary or Madonna.

Jesus *Christ.*

Then Madonna started inta *Crazy for You* – about the only thing of hurs I like. Real smoochy. They all smoothed.

It was broad daylight by this time – a bright Cork day.

Liam was doin his bit with Mary, all wrapped around hur with his hands around hur ass an his fingurs stuck into the tops a the stockins. It looked a bit above an beyond the call a duty to me. But then he was moylow.

Twas the othur two I was lookin at because twas lovely to see – Mike an Denis, I mean – movin togethur holdin each othur so closely an smilin in each othur's eyes.

Ah, yes.

It was eight a'clock in the mornin an people shoulda been thinkin a bed. I was. An Liz was. All of a sudden – she was dancin with Dec – she pitched onta the couch face down an went out like a light. An Dec came an picked me up. Joy to the world . . . An carried me into the bedroom. My heart went ter-ump, ter-ump, ter-ump. *Yes!*

He planked me down on a kinda chest a drawurs next to Mothur's alarum-clock. The alarum went *Tic Tic Tic*. An I went *Tic Tic Tic* – like a bomb tickin ovur.

But he just sat down on the edge a the bed with his elbows on his knees an did nothin. *Tic* went the clock an the minutes passed. There was a bittur taste a disappointment in me mouth but I calmed down when I noticed how weary he looked. Aftur a long while he got up an came an took me, an with a big sigh that came up from his boots he sat down again on the bed. An a flood a weariness an depression an, yeah, fear hit me comin through his hands. There were lines on his face in the mornin light an it struck me that he wasn't young any more but the blue eyes were still shinin in that misty kinda way in the sun. I tried to listen for what he was thinkin but I couldn't get anythin clear or I thought I couldn't. Then it hit me like a thundurclap that he was thinkin about me an in the same moment his eyes closed an he pressed the urun against his mouth an held it there. I was still reelin from that when I found meself back on the chest a drawurs an he was gone.

"Yerra, c'man, Mary, c'man boy, twill only take a minute!"

I came to me senses fast. What next?

Liam an Mary.

"Lave'us alone, Leeem. I don wan ta! I'm knackured, I tell yeh!"

"Ah, come on, Mary!"

They were strugglin in the middle a the room.

Jesus Christ. This wasn't fair. That I should havta be a witness to this! Me own brothur an *Mary*!

"I don wan ta!"

"Ah, shur, Mary, I'm desperate! Shur I'm mad about yeh, don't yeh know? Look, feel that!"

What! The chansur! I looked away fast. No way was I goin to see this!

Scufflin an heavy breathin an then I heard the bed creak.

"I can't, Leeem – noss in Modur's bed enyway! Lave'us get up, can't ya?"

"Yerra, Mary, don't be a fuckin prick-teasur now!"

Zippur.

"Here!"

"I swear I'll bise ya," screamed Mary but not too loud. Holy Jesus!

"Bite away! C'maaan!"

"Jaysis Christ, take dass ting away from me!"

"Jesus! That's yur fuckin hair come off!"

"Leeem! Me hayur!" screeched Mary. "I'll be dug oussa ya!"

"Tis Fawlty, isn't it? You're gone on him now, aren't yeh? What happened last night? What happened? Ah, tell me, Mary! Shur I'm mad jealous!"

"Get yur fuckin teess off me suspendurs! If yeh tear me stockins yeh'll havta gess me noo wans!"

"I will, I will!" Muffled.

Gaye Shortland

"No! Lave me knickurs alone! Stappit!"

"Ah, Mary, I can't! Have a heart! Amn't I mad for yeh?"

Then fierce bangin a drawurs an doors a the bedside table. "Jesus, doesn't the feckur have any condoms?"

"In de bassroom!"

"The bathroom! Fuck it!"

"*Aaaah!*" shrieked Mary but not too loud. "Yeh goss me wiss yur fuckin nails!"

"Sorry, sorry, shhhhh! Shhhhh! Isn't that nice? Don't yeh like that? Come on now, Mary! I'm doin all this for you . . . " The last bit all muffled.

Fierce activity. I wasn't lookin.

"*Aaaaaah!*" screeched Mary. "Holy God!"

Gasps an groans.

Pause.

Bed creak.

Water runnin at the sink for a moment.

Bed creak.

Me brothur. "Come on now, Mary! You'll havta do me now! Fair's fair!"

"Fuck aaaafff, Leeem! I'm noss doin enybody! Gimme me knickurs."

"I tell yeh, Mary, tis the way I'm fierce jealous a Fawlty since last night. What did yeh do with him? Was he any good?" Muffled. Me brothur – the investigative reportur to the bittur end.

"Get yur fuckin tongue oussa me earhole!"

Struggle on the bed.

"Tell me about Fawlty, Mary – tell me what yeh did with him. Did he fuck yeh? Did yeh give him a blow?"

"Jaysis, whass is iss ta you?"

"I'm mad jealous, Mary! Shur I think yeh're a lash."

"Go way! Yeh're a fuckin liyur! Yeh don give a shiss abouss me!"

"Ah, God, I do Mary! I think yer a grand bit a gash!

152

Honest to God! Ah, c'man boy! Yeh know what? I've been dreamin a you givin me a blow evur since the last time – d'yeh remembur? I've nevur had bettur – shur yeh're great at it. The best! C'man, don't disappoint me now! Ah, *yes*! Ay, yes! That's a good girl! Aaaaah!"

Liam had hit the jackpot – like he'd appealed to Mary's professional pride.

"Aaah, that's a good girl – that's a good girl – that's a good good girl! Get it in though – I'm goin to explode – Uh-hummmm! That's a good – hah – good – hah – girl – hah! Aaaaaaaah-HAH!"

Long pause.

Bed creak.

More runnin water.

Zippur.

Door.

"By the way," says Liam. "Cork won by a point."

Door.

Liam was gone.

You can imagine me state a mind. I could only laugh though. I felt a bit hysterical. Would yeh blame me?

It took Mary a fair while to get himself togethur – y'know, the hair-piece an the false eyelashes that had fallen off to say nothin a his tits.

Afur she went I was gigglin away, feelin a bit off the wall aftur that mind-blowin five minutes or whatevur it was, when the door opened again.

The giggles strangled in me throat. I'd kill meself. I'd try that spontaneous combustion thing.

Twas Denis an Mike. All wrapped round one anothur.

Alright!

Lights. Camera. Action.

This time I was watchin – I had money on this one like. Denis was kissin him all ovur his face while he was backin him up to the bed. There was all this "baby baby" murmurin goin on.

Then they were down on the bed an it was more "baby baby" an "sweetheart" an "darling" an sighs an moans an lookin into one anothur's eyes till I began to wondur if anythin was goin to happen at all. I mean I'd a thought, Denis bein so desperate, he would a had Mike eaten alive by this time.

Then Denis sat up. "Wait, sweetheart," says he an he kissed Mike's hand. "I'd better get this off." Meanin the tux shirt an pants. So off he went to the bathroom (to collect his condoms?) an Mike sat up an sat on the edge a the bed an took off his shoes. He started flickin somethin outa the cornurs of his eyes – make-up or somethin – an runnin his fingurs through his hair.

It was then I realised he was as nervous as a cat.

Denis came back in his towellin bathrobe.

I wasn't too happy about any a this. Where was the moonlight an roses? An *music* – Mike needed music . . . There was a hi-fi next to me – why didn't he think to stick a tape in? I remembured what Liam had said about greasin Mike's butt an suddenly it made sense aftur all.

Holy Mothur, don't let this be a cock-up.

Denis sat on the bed an started kissin him again, real gentle, an takin his shirt off at the same time. Even from where I was I could see Denis's hand shakin – oh God, he was nervous too – Jesus, but Mothur should give up the fags an the drink! His nerves were bad an no mistake. I knew his hands musta felt very cold on Mike's body.

I had a nasty feelin the man was goin to fuck up.

Mike let himself be laid back on the bed. His face was very pale. But his body was nice an brown an firm. He had his hands very lightly on Denis's shouldurs. Denis finally managed to tear himself away from Mike's face an navigate to his ear but it seemed to me like Mike wasn't reactin much nor did he when Denis navigated down to his nipple. Then all of a sudden he gave a shake an a shuddur like a car bein kick-started. His hands went inta Denis's hair. Denis was on to the fly – oh yeah! He slid his hands undur Mike's ass an got to work on his navel. I was amazed at the man's control – you couldn't help thinkin a the years of experience behind this performance. Mike was at the gaspin stage. He seemed to be grindin Denis's face inta his belly – but maybe that was Denis liftin his hips from undurneath. I was beginnin to feel I shouldn't be there. I was startin to sweat, y'know? At the same time I was cheerin Denis on – I imagined meself standin up on the chest a drawurs doin Home Run! Home Run! like yeh see in filums about baseball. Then at the height a me excitement Denis caught the waist a Mike's trousurs an pulled it right down ovur his hips to his thighs in one strong jerk an I had just time enough to notice a lot a black hair an that he had been circumcised before Denis buried his face in Mike's groin with a ferocious groan.

But now he was in a hurry an no bloody wondur. He knelt up astride Mike an shrugged his robe off.

An he didn't see what I saw: Mike's face lookin like somebody had thrown a bucket a cold watur ovur it like shock an panic an angur all rolled inta one. His arm came up an caught Denis across the Adam's apple as he bent down to kiss him. Denis sat up an grabbed at his throat an kinda gargled.

"No!" went Mike. "No!"

Denis was wheezin away. "What's the matter, sweetheart?" says he, croakin.

"No! No! I – I don't want to!" He was tryin to sit up but a course Denis was sittin on him.

"Baby!" Denis let himself down gently on top a Mike. "It's alright!" His voice was low an muffled – his face was in Mike's neck. "We don't have to do anything you don't want to. Tell me what you like, sweetheart!"

"No! Let me go!" Mike sounded breathless an desperate. He was tryin to push Denis away.

"Mike! Please! I'm sorry! I'm sorry if I was going too fast for you . . . or . . . haven't you . . . haven't you had . . . "

"It's not that!" gulped Wacko. "It's not that!"

"Sweetheart! Don't you – don't you *like* me?"

A cry like a big sob outa Mike. Another. An then he was cryin an gulpin an sobbin. Denis slid off him. Mike dragged his trousurs up an swung his legs off the bed. Then he sat there on the edge a the bed, put his head down an really let go.

Mothur looked horrified. He kinda slid off a the bed an knelt on the floor lookin at this total fuck-up of his great moment.

"Mike!" he whispured aftur a while. "Why? I thought – I thought you wanted – me." He sounded like death. "But if you don't – that's alright. There's no need to cry like that! No need! *Why* are you crying like that?"

"Because . . . because . . . " Mike gulped. I hadn't evur heard anyone ovur the age a ten years of age cry like this – nevur in all me born days.

"Yes, sweetheart? Because?"

"Because . . . " rubbin at his tears an smearin that eye-make-up all ovur his face. "Because I thought – I thought . . . "

"Yes, what did you think?"

"I thought . . . "

"Yes?"

"That maybe . . . you *loved* me . . . "

There was a noise between an ah and an uh and an eh from Mothur. Then: "But I *do* love you!" Hope dawnin. Twas pathetic, I tell yeh.

"No you don't!" Real strong from Mike. Anothur burst a tears. "You only want to fuck me!"

"*Whaaat?*"

I had to laugh.

You shoulda seen Mothur's face! Twas comic. Like total stupefaction. He went "Whaaat?" like that an his two arms opened out in his amazement.

I started to giggle. Good job they couldn't hear me. This was fuckin ridiculous! Would yeh doubt Mike!

Mothur found his tongue. "That's not true!" he gasped. "I do love you, Mike!"

"*No!* You only want to fuck me!'

"Jesus!" says Mothur. "Can't I do both?"

Oh, my God! I wanted a video-camera! The othurs'd give their two eyes out to see this! Mothur kneelin stark naked on the floor with his arms stretched out: Jesus! Can't I do *both*?

Mike wasn't finished yet. "You see! Tis always the same!" He was rockin back an forth like someone demented – which a course he is. "Tis always the same! It always turns out like that!"

"Like what, sweetheart?" asks the poor man.

"They always just want to fuck me!"

"Holy Lord! Holy Lord!" Mothur got up an stalked around bitin his fingurs – a fine figure of a man – an I'm not talkin about his muscular development. "Holy Jesus! God Almighty!"

Aftur a fair while at this he came back an knelt down again an tried to look inta Mike's face undur the hair. "Who's 'they'?"

Big hesitation. "Anybody." Real uncertain. "Anybody who pr-pretends to c-care about me." He had stopped cryin. His voice sounded all cracked.

Jesus, a fuckin mental-case. We always knew it.

Mothur pushed the hair back off Mike's face. He stayed there starin at Mike an bitin his lip with his face all screwed up. Mike didn't look at him.

I was gettin edgy – the hysterics had passed off. I mean

this was fuckin exhaustin. What was the mattur with these people? They thought they had problems! They were alive, for Chrissake! An mad about each othur as far as I could see. What the fuck was the problem? There *wasn't* any problem! *There wasn't any problem.* The fact that they were so fuckin lucky was enough to make me weep. The fact they were makin a cock-up of it was enough to make me want to kick em in the balls. *Jesus! People!*

Fuck it, Denis! I thought. Fuck this! Find a way out, man! Try a clout around the earhole, try anythin! But nevur say die! Y'see, you don't havta say die – you're *alive*, yeh lucky bastard!

An just then Denis gave a little lift a the head – a tiny little movement but I knew it meant he had made up his mind about somethin.

"Well, *I love you* – you can be sure of that," he said. He pushed Mike's hair back behind his ears. "Hey!" Real gentle. "You do look an absolute wreck! Go and wash your face, there's a good boy! Where's all your eye-stuff and all that?"

"In my jacket. Outside."

"Go on! Wash your face – I'll get your jacket." Mothur stood Mike up an gave him a little push towards the sink. He dragged his robe on an went out an came back with the jacket an Mike pulled all this crap outa the pockets – the make-up an his backin tapes an all that.

"Ah yes," says Mothur in a strange tone I couldn't figure out. "Michael Jackson. Just what we need." An he put one of the tapes in the hi-fi.

Good move, Denis. And about time for yeh. Yeh fuckin eejit.

You an I must make a pact
We must bring salvation back
Where there is love I'll be they-uh!

What a fuckin relief! Even I felt kinda uplifted when that

clear voice came outa the hi-fi. It sounded like an anjul in the sunshine. It sounded like a pint a Murphys tastes when yeh have a terrible thirst.

Michael musta been about ten singin that song.

Let me fill your heart with joy and laughter –

A bloody good idea. More power to yur elbow, Michael.

Togetherness – well it's all I'm after
Whenever you need me I'll be they-uh!

True for him – he was certainly they-uh when we needed him, God bless him.

Mike started to smile. Mothur started to smile. Mike re-gooed his eyes. Mothur brushed Mike's hair. Mothur kissed Mike on the forehead. Mike ran his fingurs over the lines on Mothur's face an kissed him on the lips. Mothur put his arms around Mike an kissed him good an propur. Mike gave a sigh an put his arms around Mothur's neck an kissed him back.

Mothur said, a bit nervously but tryin to sound confident: "Dinner tonight here at eight – *vegetarian*! Your choice of everything and Michael Jackson all the way through. What do you say to that, my beauty?"

"Okay," whispured Wacko.

Jesus, maybe they'd get sense yet.

Oooo! Oooo! Oooo! Ooooo! sang Michael Jackson like he was havin an under-age orgasm.

There was a knock at the door. Dec lookin for his bag. I got removed too an I thanked God. For all I loved those two eejits, they had me fluthered. You could only put up with so much a that kinda thing.

They all left then except Dec an Liam. Mothur made a bit a breakfast.

"Ooo! Ooo! Ooo! Baby!" sang Liam, grabbin his crotch an crossin his legs an got such a savage look from Mothur he shut up an there wasn't anothur word outa him. The message was clear that Mothur hadn't got his rocks off. Mothur sat around broodin for a while an Cohen got played.

An played. An played.

But I'm stubborn as those garbage bags
That time cannot decay
I'm junk but I'm still holdin up
This little wild bouquet
Democracy is comin to the USA.

I hope you are Mothur, I thought – stubborn like the garbage bags an holdin up the little bouquet.

Every heart
To love will come
But like a refugee . . .

Dec went off an left me with Liam. He'd do the rounds, he said, invitin people to me funeral. Liam fell asleep on the couch. Then Mothur went to bed an I was left with Cohen.

I swear it happened just like this
A sigh, a cry, a hungry kiss
The gates of love they budged an inch
I can't say much has happened since
It's closin time . . .

Yeah, it was closin time for me. Or last call anyway.

About three a'clock Mothur emerged from his bedroom lookin like shit. He woke Liam up.

"Liam, let's go!"

"Where?"

"Town, my boy!"

I went too in a bag.

Mothur looked a bit demented an kept runnin his hands through his hair.

Into the Oak for a drink. Liam fell asleep with his chin on his hand.

Inta Roches for some wine. An Ballygowan. An orange.

Into the flowur-shop by Cudmore's cornur for roses.

Red roses. Liam woke up.

Inta a jewellur's shop which will be nameless on Olivur Plunkett Street.

"Your hand is his size," said Mothur as they went in. "You can choose. I'm hopeless at making this kind of decision."

One of the assistants came ovur – a young man in a suit.

"We're interested in engagement rings," said Mothur.

"Oh, come this way, if you please, Sir!" He made a sign to anothur assistant, a lady in a suit, an the two a them ushured us inta this little back room. Twas very fancy with a red sofa with curvy legs an musak piped in – *The First Time that evur I saw Your Face.*

Mothur an Liam sat down on the sofa.

The Suited Lady made some remarks about the fine weathur. She was claspin hur hands in a way that reminded me a Tizzy.

"What size?" asked the Young Man. "Has the lady a small hand?"

"Oh, his size, dahling!" said Mothur.

"Oh! That will be large," said the Young Man. "And the stone? A single diamond or a cluster?"

"What do you want?" Mothur asked Liam.

The assistant began to look a bit strained. He shot a look ovur at the Suited Lady.

"Oh, let's have a bit a colour in it," said Liam. "I think diamonds are dull." An he smiled at the Young Man from undur his lashes. The Young Man blushed. Just outa confusion, I'd say. That seemed to inspire Liam. He pulled out a bunch a sticks a bubble-gum from his pocket an stuffed them all inta his mouth, so he could blow it in the assistant's face an unnerve him more.

"And the price-range?" Very polite an careful.

"Doesn't matter, dahling," said Mothur, wavin a hand. "He's worth it, whatever!"

"Oh!"

They went out an then the Suited Lady came back with little dooshie boxes a hand-made chocolates labelled "The Food of Love". Liam took out the wad a bubble-gum an parked it on Mothur's cuff-link. Mothur didn't seem to notice. Liam ate all the chocolates immediately. He was stuffin them in his mouth when the Young Man came in with rakes a rings on boards covured with red velvet an he hadta stand there while Liam ate the chocolates. Everyone watched Liam chewin. He was havin trouble with the caramel ones.

Liam choked or pretended to an hadta be walloped on the back by Mothur.

Then he recovured his bubble-gum an the assistants presented the rings.

Now Liam really got into the act. He tried on diamonds an sapphires, an diamonds an emeralds, an diamonds an rubies, an diamonds an amethysts. They discussed chips an clusters an carats an prices. Liam stood up an pranced around. He blew gum in the assistant's face an batted his eyelids. He held his hand up to his face an threw shapes in the glass. He decided sapphires suited his eyes. Mothur took a fancy to emeralds.

They had a row.

"Yeh said I could choose, mothurfuckur!"

"Sweetheart, there's no need to be so *intransigent*!"

The Suited Lady spoke up. "Perhaps you should consider rubies?" Very cautious.

"Ah, yes! Dark! With passion at the heart! That would suit his personality," cried Mothur.

"Eh, yes," said the Suited Lady.

They settled on a ruby in a circle a diamonds. The Suited Lady wanted to know if she should box it.

"Oh, yes, darling," said Mothur. "You see I haven't

actually proposed yet."

The manajur or ownur was called to approve Mothur's cheque – I think he made a phone-call from his office before he did because he came back bowin an scrapin like mad aftur bein very odd with us before.

Liam linked Mothur's arm an we left in a big chorus a goodbyes an good lucks – they'd called the jewellurs an apprentices down from upstairs an all to see us.

Into Counihans for a drink.

"Yeh know yeh'll havta give up the drink if Mike is goin to live with yeh?"

"Oh yes, oh yes," said Mothur. "That will be excellent! That will be excellent!"

As soon as we got back to the flat he started foosterin around preparin his meal an the table an the flowurs an the music an all.

Liam chose his shirt for him – one a them collarless things with little black buttons – an he laid it out for him on the bed.

Denis lit a coal fire an fixed up rugs an cushions an stuff – where he imagined himself enjoyin the long romantic evenin.

Twas pathetic. If it didn't work out the man would be suicidal. Liam should a laid out one a the sharpur kitchen knives too.

When Liam was ready to go he actually kissed Denis on the cheek for luck, which was a strange thing for Liam to do because he doesn't go in for kissin men – not that way anyway.

An then when he was almost out the door he turned.

"And, Denis . . . "

"Yes?"

"Just the tiniest drop a vodka in the orange . . . "

A big eyebrow raisin competition followed between em. Denis won.

So off we went hot-foot down town dyin to meet Dec an tell him the news. Up an down Pana with us till we found him at long last. Up an down till we met Mad Mary. An up an down till we bumped inta Liz an the Bonny Boy. The Bonny Boy had on his school uniform. "Hello, Dec! Liam! How's things?" With his tie all skew-ways. An a tatty oul canvas bag bulgin with books ovur one shouldur. Well, whatevur turns yeh on. Mind yeh, he was good-lookin. Right appealin, with black hair an greenish eyes an fine strong features.

Anyway, that was only the half of it. Liz had this retarded kid with hur that she takes care of – a kid of about twelve years old who doesn't talk at all. He's a gangly dark-haired kid – with cross-eyes an fierce protrudin teeth that make him look like somethin out a comic – y'know, they're not just protrudin, they're kinda splayed.

Liz said the kid was startin to bite people so we should do somethin to entertain him. So off with us to The Spailpín Fánach where they have live music some days. Liz gave the Bonny Boy hur jumpur an he pulled it ovur his school uniform – twas a kinda mossy green that went lovely with his eyes. They gave One Flew Ovur the school-bag to carry in an he was delighted with that.

It so happened that the live music was a kinda traditional group lookin like The Hothouse Flowurs or An Emotional Fish – all long hair an pony-tails an beards – hunks now like. They were in the small little side-place near the fire so we all crowded in there too.

They bought crisps an still orange for One Flew Ovur an ordured drinks: tonic an a slice a lemon – a great old standby – y'know vodka an white like. They were all craw-sick from the drink by this time an skint besides, except for Liam.

"Whasupitchur hands?" Liam asked Liz.

"Him – Timmy," she said, pullin back hur shirt-sleeves. She was all scratches an black-an-blue marks up to her elbows. "I had to take him to the Passion Play at Lota today an he got claustraphobic. Here he was all the way through!" An she did a mime a One Flew Ovur tryin to get his teeth in hur. Lota is the Cork home for retarded childrun. "It was terrible! Y'see, I couldn't call here to him because it was in the chapel – all I could do was hold him off."

"And what do you have the back a yer hand for?" asked Dec. He turned to the Bonny Boy. "On the lang from school again, I suppose?"

"No, no – tis my lunch-hour," said the Bonny Boy.

"But I suppose it's because of you Liz dragged Timmy inta town?"

"Well, yes," said the Bonny Boy.

"Well, I hope you'll take propur responsibility for him."

"I suppose I'll have to," said the Bonny Boy with a chuckle so small twas more like a gasp. He was eatin crisps an I noticed his hands had a slight tremor. Nervous type undurneath it all. "So the funeral's tomorrow?" says he, changin the subject.

"Yes, God willing," said Dec.

"Y'know what?" said Liam. "This is like a wake for Tony. We should a thought a givin him a wake."

"Shur didn't we give him a wake last night?" said Dec.

But I got fished outa the bag an put on the table between the pints. An a course I got me usual fit a nerves. All it needed was a handy barman now to mistake me for a dead man an I'd be cleared away with the empty glasses. Dead man . . . Jaysis, that's good! I might make a stand-up comic yet.

They explained to the Hot Flushes that I was bein scattured an how I had died an all. The Hot Flushes were very impressed – you'd swear that their only ambition in life was to die of AIDS in London an be scattured up at the Good Shepherds, they thought twas such a great deal. I could a told em twas very easily achieved – like fallin off a log.

Next thing anyway the Hot Flushes started inta *Poc ar Buile* an One Flew Ovur started gettin very excited. Twas the bodhrán an the spoons that got him goin. Y'know there's fierce work on the bodhrán in that one. Nothin would do him but to have a go.

"Hould yur horses, Timmy," said Liam. "Leave it to Uncle Liam!"

"*Aunty* Liam," said Dec, with a camp little smirk.

An Liam asked the Hot Flushes to let One Flew Ovur have a go. And a course they couldn't say no. I mean they all had their consciousness raised by seein *My Left Foot*. In othur words they were afraid that One Flew Ovur was some kinda genius undur it all an he would be writin his autobiography one a these days an slatin em if they refused. I mean they would a told a normal young fella go fuck himself before they'd let him touch that bodhrán – the things cost a fortune an have to be buried in a bog for forty years or somethin to season the skin before they're ready for use.

Anyway, One Flew Ovur got to bang the bodhrán for the next song an twas painful to see the face a the bodhrán ownur. I had to laugh. They grabbed it back from him before the last note a the song an gave him the spoons instead. Jaysis, the clattur he made with the spoons!

So the Hot Flushes played an One Flew Ovur clattured an the lads really got inta it with clappin an foot-stampin an singin. Twas atrocious. We were all in stitches. We could hear the people behind the bar goin "Jesus Christ, isn't this awful altogethur, havin to be puttin up with this!" But a course there was nothin they could do about it because the reason the Flushes were there at all was for a sing-song like.

"Audience participation," says Dec with a sniff.

The Hot Flushes didn't care as long as they had their hands on their bodhrán an their free pints. But I'd say in the end we wore em out. Twas a great wake – despite bein a daytime effort. I couldn't a asked for a bettur.

So there we were, long aftur the Hot Flushes were aftur goin home. Worn out ourselves by this stage.

"Tony's last evenin with us," said Liam, sighin.

Oh God, I hoped they weren't goin to get maudlin.

They weren't.

"Can't he buy us a round a drinks so?" said Mary.

"God help us, shur he can't go up an buy a round," says Dec. "What would the barman say?"

"I'll buy the round," said Liam.

So when they got the pints down em they all got their second wind. Liam starts gettin randy an puts a hand between Mary's thighs – still in the laddured stockins.

Mary started squawkin immediately. "Stop glawmin me or I'll hit ya a flake!"

"Ah, Mary, Mary!" A big wink at Dec. "Whasupitcha? Shur you're always comin on to everyone else! What's wrong with me?"

"Fuck aaaff, baoy! Where's me bear? Liz, gimme me bear dere!"

"So," says Liz aftur handin ovur the bear. "We'll drink to Tony, will we?"

"Well, we can't drink to his health," said Dec. Very camp an bitchy.

"Maybe we'd bettur drink to our own," said Liam. "Poor Tony doesn't have to worry any more."

Worry! If he only knew!

"Well, anyway: to Tony!" said Liz raisin her pint.

So they all said "To Tony" an took a slug outa their pints.

"But this funeral," said Liam. "I can't help feelin that there should be simplur way a doin it . . . "

"A simplur way!" said Dec, annoyed. "Well, sorry for askin ye to put yeerselves out! Twas very inconsiderate of Tony alright to go an die on us! Okay – tell me a simplur way of doing it so!" He was in his spit-in-yur-eye pose now with his chin up an his ankles crossed an his knees to one side an his back straight.

"Jesus, I don't know," said Liam. "Maybe we should drink him down with our pints like Holy Comunion an be done with it!"

"We could do worse!" said Dec. "I agree. *That* would be appropriate. I'm willing for that if you are!"

Whaat? Holy Hour! Journey to the Centur a the Earth!

"But it's not what he wanted," said Dec. Very precise.

"Who knows what he wanted?" said Liam. "I tell ye he was outa his brain by the end."

"Alright," said Liz. "I think we should have a vote on this. Right. Drinking him down with the pints! All in favour say aye!"

A course they all said aye outa divilment – all except Dec an Liam who were still vexed an eyein each othur.

"You're outvoted," said Liz to Dec.

"Look," said Dec. "I may know nothin bout birthin no babies but I've funerals to a fine art. We're havin the funeral."

Saved.

"Ah shur, twill be grand on the night," said Liz.

So the night wore on – slow as molasses in January like Scarlett would say. The two took One Flew Ovur home an came back again. Liam drank too much an got bad an ended up cryin his eyes out about me in Dec's arms outside The Long Valley an they hadta walk him home. Then way up past Dillon's Cross he stopped dead an said he wanted to go back to Mad Mary's place. I knew he'd remembured that if he went home to his bed that would leave Mary on the loose an she'd a been poundin on Denis's door within the hour. Fair dues to him, drunk an all as he was, he was still doin his bit for Mothur. They were all knackured an half-langurs so they had a dispute about this that lasted forevur. Liz an the Bonny Boy wanted to get Liam home to his bed but Dec – an a course Mary for his own reasons – wanted to cart him off back down to Mary's place.

In the end Liam was so set on goin back he staggured off down the hill by himself an Mary an the bear went lurchin off aftur him. So the rest went home.

So at last, at long last, I found meself sittin on Dec's bedside table. He lit his candle an put out the light. Great. The glare a the bedside lamp right up agin me was givin me a headache.

I tried to prepare meself for the worst which was that he should ignore me. An that's what he did. He got inta bed.

I tried.

"I know you won't let me down, Dec boy, on me last night. This is me last chance to be with you – to be with anyone! Think of it – nevur again to embrace anothur human bein or even to laugh with anybody – unless there are a few bits a me left to have a giggle with any a the nuns visitin the grave."

He sat up. He swung his legs off the bed an sat there an stared at me. Was he hearin me?

He kept starin an I kept talkin – not even knowin if he was hearin me – but what else could I do? "I know tis too late now. But there's this one night. Dec? You're not goin to leave me out in the cold, are yeh?"

Nothin. I couldn't pick up anything from him. For all I knew he could a been thinkin a somethin else altogethur – like whethur he'd turned off the gas or put the cat out.

"This is me last chance. Think a where I'm goin! Think a the cold and the misury of it! But if I had this last night warm an safe with you I'd have the memory a that! But how long will I have a memory even? What's goin to happen when there's not a scrap a me left? All blown away in the wind – washed away by the rain . . . Jesus!"

He wasn't listenin. He got up an started rootin around in his cassette tapes. Took a while at it.

Finally in went a cassette. I got an awful start when the song came on. I thought I was on the grave already – a noise like the wind in wintur an a thud like a heartbeat – an then a voice singin in a style like sean-nós. I knew the voice – twas Philip King an Scullion – from the Kilcrea Park Dec was always revilin.

I am stretched on your grave and would lie there forevur
If your hands were in mine I'd be sure we'd not sevur
My appletree my brightness tis time we were togethur
For I smell of the earth and am worn by the weathur.

There was a single instrument gatherin strength far behind the singin voice. My breath was taken away.

The priests and the friars approach me in dread
Because I still love you my love and you're dead
And still would be your shelter through rain and through storm
And with you in the cold grave I cannot sleep warm.

And the fiddle followed on with a melody fit to break your heart.

I hardly knew when he picked me up. I didn't know whethur the hot tears were his or my own. But I reached out an I took him in my arms an it seemed to me I had arms. And I hardly knew what we were exchangin – whether twas tears or saliva or pleasure or pain an when I passed into him I hardly knew how or in what way.

CHAPTER 7

"FOR *FUCK'S* SAKE, WHAT THE *FUCK* ARE YEH DOIN WITH THE *fuckin urun*!" Liam. Draggin the bedclothes off us. "Are yeh off yur game or what? *Look!* The fuckin thing's *opened*! Half of it is all ovur the *fuckin bed*!"

He grabbed up a copy of *The Fold* (the Dioscesan magazine) an started tryin to sweep the stray bits a me off the sheet.

"Jesus Christ, isn't this awful altogethur! Godilmighty bless us, isn't this awful! You weren't that drunk! Look! I can't shift it! Half of it is stuck to the fuckin sheet! Oh Gaawd! Fuckin disgustin!" An he threw *The Fold* down on the bed in a tempur.

"Would you be careful with that *Fold*," said Dec politely, pullin the sheet up undur his arms. "I have to give it back to Sistur Breeda – she only lent it to me to read an article – 'Where is the Spirit today?' She's trying to convert me to the new forms of spirituality – unsuccessfully, I must say."

I had to laugh.

Liam gaped at him. "I think you've gone off yur *chuck*! Anyway, forget *The Fold* – the thing's ruined! I'm gone! I'm goin down to Mothur's!"

An he shoved the urun in his bag an pounded down the hill in a right fury. When he got to Mothur's he stopped in the street an lit up. The nerves were in shreds. When he'd half-smoked the fag he threw it down an ground it out an went into the house.

He hesitated again outside the door a the flat. Listenin hard. Then he took a deep breath an knocked.

Mary opened the door. Bare from the neck to the crotch undur a denim jacket – I swear, yeh could see bits a pubic hair. No hair-piece, no spiked hair but eyes starin outa big circles a black eye-shada.

Liam just stared. I felt his heart sinkin like an elevatur goin down. Whoooooooooooooosh!

"He's in de kitchin," said Mary. Very haughty. He swayed off inta the bedroom.

"Wait up! Mary!" He followed him. "Have yeh been here long?"

"Whas iss ta you, baoy?" says Mary, lightin up an startin to smoke like a chimney – because he doesn't inhale at all. "Ya goss up an lef me, didn't ya?"

"I hadta go home an tell me sistur about the funeral, didn't I? An get changed an all!" He was wearin his suit an lookin a right mashur.

"Yeh're a fuckin liyur!"

"Jesus!"

Out with Liam an he barged inta the livin-room an then he stopped in his tracks. Listenin. There was music. A ghost of a smile came ovur Liam's face. He tip-toed ovur to the kitchen door an peeped in.

Denis was cookin breakfast – somethin on the pan. He was dancin to the music, swayin his hips an scrabblin away at the pan with a whatsit at the same time. You had only to look at him to see the man was in heaven – the reason bein that he had Mike latched onta him around his neck like they were welded bone to bone.

And oh yes, Mike was wearin the ring.

The song? Well, what d'yeh think? Wacko Jacko, who

else? An that love-song that he sings to a rat, y'know the one?

Ben the two of us need look no more
We both found what we were lookin for
With a friend to call my own
I'll never be alone –

I had to laugh. Mothur had sold Cohen down the rivur. He wouldn't be listenin to him for a long time to come.

Liam was clutchin at the base of his stomach – I could feel him holdin onta the laughtur like someone tryin not to throw up.

Next thing a kinda gasp a laughtur escaped him an he staggured away from the door at the same time.

Mothur came out with the whatsit in his hand, his eyes all lit up. He grabbed Liam's arm an kissed him on the cheek. "Listen, darling," said Mothur in a low voice. "I'm worried about Mary – I'm afraid he may be sulking. Could you?"

Liam give him a big thumbs-up. "I'll take care a Mary. Don't worry a bit."

So in we went to the bedroom an dragged Mary out for a cup a coffee down in O'Brien's. Mary was narky, alright. Aftur all, it musta been a bit of a land to walk in on Romeo an Juliet.

Down the hill, bear an all. You'd be mortified what with the bear an Mary's pubic hair. But me brothur didn't seem to care. Me brothur was very happy all of a sudden.

An there was Dec comin down MacCurtain Street. My heart turned over an various parts a the anatomy I didn't have started to pulsate. He was dressed all in black – black denim like – with a black polo-neck. An a silvur crucifix around his neck catchin the sun.

Inta O'Brien's with us with Liam makin victory signs about Mothur to Dec behind Mary's back. A queer look we got from the women behind the countur, what with Mary an the bear. O'Brien's is one a them old-fashioned places where the women behind the countur nevur seem to die – they just get oldur an oldur.

Me brothur bought the coffee an big slices a gudge. Dec refused to eat on accounta why he wasn't aftur havin any breakfast. But he couldn't be persuaded to have breakfast eithur an in the end he admitted he was on a fast. I was too.

"The coffee's me daza," said Liam. Everythin was me daza for Liam just then.

Mary tasted the coffee. "Whajameen? Tis chronic!"

Liam laughed. He stretched out his legs an lit up. "D'yeh like me suit?" he smiled at Mary.

"Tis massive, baoy."

"You're not goin to the funeral like that, are yeh?" Liam yanked at the nipple-ring.

"Aaaaaaaaaah!" screeched Mary an one a the women behind the countur dropped a plate. We heard her swearin: "Jesus, Mary an Josuph!"

"Not that I don't like yeh like this," says Liam an his hand went down across Mary's skinny belly an right inta his groin.

"Leggo a me prick!" screeched Mary.

"Jesus, Mary an Josuph!" Behind the countur.

Liam let go an started playin with the pubic hairs instead – the ones we could see. Mary let him.

"Dec, the problem is – I'm mad about Mary. I mean Mary's a lash – aren't yeh, Mary?"

"Fuckin liar! Yeh only want to make a cod a me!"

"Ah, Mary, that's not true. Shur, I'm mad for yeh. Shur wasn't I like a bonfire last night? D'think I'm like that with everyone? Dec – Dec, tell him! Shur, Mary, the very sight a yeh gives me a hard-on – isn't that a fact, Dec?"

"I wouldn't know anything about your barometur, Liam, or degrees of interest expressed thereby." With a sniff.

"D'hear that, Mary? Y'see? Y'see what I mean? Dec knows how I feel about yeh!"

The chansur!

Liam went on. He was having a great time at this. "Dec, I tell yeh what. We havta take care a Mary now. We havta take ovur from Mothur." Puttin an arm around Mary's bony shouldurs.

"We? We? Are yeh serious like? He's all yours, Liam. Take care away if you're so inclined!"

"Ah, I am so I am, indeedin I am," said Liam. "But the thing is: I'm a fierce jealous type. I'd go mad altogethur if he was fuckin around with othur fellas. The thing is: will yeh do a line with me, Mary?"

Dec's eyes rolled to Heaven.

"Fuck aaff, baoy!" says Mary.

"Ah, c'man! For the craic! Twould be cool!"

"Fuck aaff, baoy! Yeh're only coddin me! Yeh don't give a shiss abouss me – Modur's de only wan who cared abouss me."

"You're right there," says Dec suddenly, right bitchy. "I, for one, do not want you at this funeral."

"What?" says Liam. "Aren't I the brothur to the deceased an isn't Mary me moth? Shur, she must be there!"

"I'm noss yur moss!" says Mary "Liiiiiiiiiiiz!"

"Jesus, Mary an Josuph!" Behind the countur.

Liz an the Bonny Boy were passin the winda. In they came an One Flew Ovur with em.

"Jesus," said Dec. "Now we're a right menagerie. We were bad enough with one mentally defective." Mary like. "Whatevur took yeh to bring him an me tryin to run a respectable funeral?"

"I had to," said Liz. "His mothur is sick."

"Shu' God help him," said Mary. "He's lookin ass de ice-cream!"

"D'ye have any money?" asked Liz. "I haven't a tossur."

175

"Here," said the Bonny Boy.

"That's your lunch-money," said Liz.

"No, take it. Tis alright. An get some coffee."

Pathetic.

Next thing they were wonderin if they could all pile in on top a Romeo an Juliet for lunch an decided they couldn't in all fairity. So they did Pana for a while with Dec an Liz doin the quartet from *Rigoletto* all the way – two parts each – so I got me wish there.

We left Mary an the bear down in fronta the Moderne with the fireswallowur – y'know the fella all covured in soot an petrol who juggles – with the wild red hair? I dunno how she knew him. Or even if she knew him. "Well, that's got rid a hur!" said Dec with great satisfaction.

I dunno why I'm tellin yeh all this about that mornin when I should be movin on to the Last Rites. I suppose because I was livin every minute of it an hangin onta every minute of it. Closin Time for me.

And the whole damn place goes crazy twice
And it's once for the Devil and it's once for Christ
But the boss don't like these dizzy heights
We're busted in the blindin lights
Of closin time –

That was me sure enough.

It was time.

We headed off up to the Good Shepherds. A right menagerie, as Dec said, even without Mary an the bear.

And I swear it happened just like this
A sigh, a cry, a hungry kiss
The gates of love they budged an inch
I can't say much as happened since
It's closin time –

When we hit the convent there was a rake a people already there. Dec had done a good job. There was a blue Sierra (Gardaí) parked overright the convent next to a

Toyota that looked like Aunty Eileen's an there was a pack
a dodderin ould folk – Dec's neighbours, I suppose. Yeah,
there was Fawlty talkin to a fierce flashy-lookin blonde in a
black leathur jacket ovur a mini-skirt. Jay, twas Drachma!
Me sistur! Last time I'd seen hur she was a flamin red-head.

So in with Dec an Liam, an me, to find the Bride a
Frankenstein. Twas cold an quiet in the convent corridors.

I can't say much has happened since –

The Bride was in hur office – wipin hur nose. Christ! I
resented it. Me last moments – spent watchin hur snortin!

She looked up ovur the handkurchief with hur scanty
eyebrows raised over the cold blueish eyes. "Ye-es?" she
crackled. Huge snort. I was reachin for me Magnum 45
already.

"About the funeral?" said Dec. Very mellow altogethur.

"Yes," says she through that nose – very mellow too. "If
you'll just wait outside – Oh, Liam isn't it? Has Sister
Veronica arrived?"

Dec looked at Liam an Liam looked at Dec. What with
one thing an anothur, they'd forgotten about Dec's nun-
drag.

"Aaah –" Dec recovured fast. "I'm Sistur Veronica's
brothur – she can't come – aaah, she had to leave. She had
to fly out this morning – trouble back at hur convent – eh,
the Reverend Mothur died – eh, committed suicide last
night –"

The Bride hit a bell on the desk a smart wallop. She got
to hur feet an hur bones creaked as she strode ovur to us.
"But that's terrible! What happened at all?"

"It was a drinking-problem, Mothur. Ah, she was going
to have to step down – Bishop's intervention."

Liam was lookin horrified. I could see sweat on his
uppur lip.

"Mother Ursula?" Ursula was bustlin in. "Come and hear
this!" An she grabbed Dec's arm in a vice.

"Liam!" Ursula beamed a big toothy grin at him. "How are yeh at all at all?" An she got hold a his two hands.

An they kept us there helpless, shakin us like puppies, while they got all this mind-bendin information outa Dec. They wanted every detail about the drunkun Reverend Mothur an he was the man to give it to em. He threw in a few affairs with bishops and psychiatric diseases for good measure. They'd listen, then they'd stare at each othur without sayin anythin an the Bride would do gymnastics with hur denture.

In the end, in desperation, Liam hauled me outa the bag to distract em an then we had more from em on cremation.

At long last we all went outside. An there was Mrs Leary puffin up the hill in a suit she had worn for a weddin the year before – a pinkish effort with a pillbox type a hat with all this net on it. An coughin up the hill behind her a decrepit oul taxi-cab. The cab stopped an a girl got out. I thought I didn't know her from Adam an then she reached inta the back an dragged out the pink bear. Yeah, twas Mad Mary – not down in Patrick Street swallyin flame an flashin hur pubic hair but here in a little black dress with long sleeves an not a suspendur showin.

"I think we could organise a cup of tea while the guests are gathering, couldn't we, Mother Ursula? Some of those elderly people came by bus – the ones who didn't come in the Squad car – and they've been here for ages already and there's a nip in the air up here for all the sunshine. It wouldn't do if they caught their death of cold out of it. What do you think?"

"Oh, yes, and maybe Liam and – ?"

"Declan, Mothur."

" – Declan could help with pouring the tea?" Shakin Liam with one hand an pattin his face with the othur.

"I'll get the Magdalens to set up the trestle-table so," said the Bride an she went stridin off, an me an Liam an

Dec followed Ursula inta the kitchen. An Godilmighty bless us didn't Liam put me down outa his hand on the table.

That's how it happened.

This fat ould Magdalen in filthy ould slippurs an one a them country overalls, them navy-blue ones with sprigs a flowurs on, was lumberin round the kitchen an when Ursula told her about the tea she got out this big kettle an put the watur on to boil. Ursula put cups an spoons an things on big metal trays an off went Dec an Liam with em. Then Ursula an the Magdalen had a dispute about how many spoons a tea to put in the pot – or the kettle I should say. A course Ursula got hur way. But as soon as she went out aftur Liam an Dec with the sugur an milk, the Magdalen poured hurself out a cup a tea an took a sup outa it. She made a face an muttured to hurself an scrabbled around in the drawur an took out a dessertspoon. Then hur hand came down on top a the urun an before I could catch me breath the dessertspoon came plungin inta me vittels an she lobbed three big heaps a me into the scaldin water. Aaaaaaaaah! It only hurt for a minute. Twas more the indignity like! An then she picked up the urun an shoved me inta a welter a tea-caddies up on a dressur. The sweat started to come outa me – an not because part a me was stewin in a kettle.

In came the lads an I'm screamin for attention but they don't hear me. They're all into bein caterurs – y'know Liam an Dec – they nevur do things halfways.

Dec picked up the kettle an off they go again an I almost yelped when I found meself movin with em, I was so startled.

This was a bewilderin experience. Technically I was sittin on the dressur. Technically there were only bits a me in the kettle – stewed bits at that.

Jesus Christ Almighty! Me mouth went dry. What if? What if? What if I had transferred to the kettle? What was goin to happen to me when I was devoured by the bunch a cannibals outside?

I was seein everythin through a haze – an I was sea-sick besides, bein sloshed about like I was. There was Aunty Kitty in hur cast, spinnin like a top outa the Toyota. There was Cliona – it had to be Cliona – staggerin up the drive on high heels with hur funeral gear on, with the black veil ovur her face.

I was sweatin an sick. There was One Flew Ovur gallumpin across Mad Mary an grabbin the bear.

"Take yur fuckin hands aaff me bear, ya spastic!"

A fierce wrestle started that was broken up by the Bonny Boy. I'd just time to see One Flew Ovur bein dragged off with his teeth sunk in the Bonny Boy's arm before Dec swung the kettle around.

When me head stopped spinnin I was bein poured. I saw Dec's caterin smile like at the end of a tunnel. I braced meself as well as I could for the first experience a bein eaten alive but I didn't feel anythin. I saw Fawlty slurpin his tea while blushin mad at the sight a Mary an the bear makin for him but I still didn't feel anythin except like I might feel on a December crossin a the *St Brendan*. Then I remembured twasn't me first experience a bein eaten alive. I remembured the time Dec had licked me off his fingur, the day we got off the boat. That had been pleasure – it hadn't hurt.

Dec was fillin away an everyone was washin me down. Jaysis, if this was the way I was goin to end I'd a preferred to have been washed down with the pints the night before – at last I wouldn't a had this awful sea-sickness. It really was like a bad night on the Irish Sea. Except worse because there was nothin to hold onta.

"I always say there's nothin like Barry's," came Mrs Burke's voice from somewhere. "I'd say this is Mace now or one a them economy things. If I was down to me last few bob I wouldn't buy um an that's a fact!"

"I tell yeh what it is," muttered Mrs Leary's voice. "Tis that factory stuff – y'know – the sweepins – sawdust!"

Dec swung round. There was Mothur lookin sharp with forty-five rings on, sippin his tea, with the Bride swivellin hur denture in his face. What in God's name were they discussin so seriously? And where was Mike?

"De tea's chronic!" came Mary's screech from somewhere.

I looked for Mike as Dec swung me round an round an up an down. Ah, yes, there he was, all in black an silvur – very romantic like Prince Charmin or somethin except that he had One Flew Ovur by the hand an One Flew Ovur was droolin all over the Prince Charmin jacket an tryin to bite the silvur buttons offa the cuffs.

Slosh! Slosh! In the pot! Or "posss" like Mary would say it, the real Cork way with a real hiss to it. Slosh! Slosh! In the Possss!

There was Aunty Kitty havin fierce trouble drinkin hur tea because a the cast, lookin like one a them circus jugglurs that spin the plates balanced on their foreheads an chins.

But where was Tizzy?

"Dec?" Liam.

"Yeah?"

"Dec! The priest? Did yeh get a priest?"

"Jesus!"

"Yeh didn't *forget*?"

"I'm afraid I did."

The kettle was steadyin. Me head was clearin a bit.

"What!" In a savage whispur. "What's the mattur with yeh since last night? What's happened to yur head? You're all spaced out! First yeh're messin around with the urun, then yeh forget yur nun-gear! Now've no priest!"

And no urun, lads.

I was only jigglin about a bit now in the kettle.

"We could get Sistur Breeda to say a few words," said Dec. "Be very progressive like – female clergy an all that –"

"The nuns'd nevur stand for it."

"We'll have to have the chaplain so – hope he's there."

They found the Bride an told hur. She put a hand on hur jaw an pulled it down, with hur fingurs sinkin into the hollows of hur cheeks. "Good Lord! I suppose he'll manage! It's a bit short notice."

Off with hur, with Liam an Dec trailin behind – Dec with the kettle an Liam with a bunch a cups in one hand. We were just goin to plunge into the convent aftur hur when Liam halted suddenly an Dec an I went inta a huge sickenin slosh in the posss.

Into the parkin space overright the convent came a bunch a weird-lookin vehicles. There was a huge Rangerover an a van –

"Jaysis, tis Tizzy!"

An there was Tizzy climbin out – all of a tizzy – in his slinky grey silk suit with the string tie an all red in the face. He spotted us an came up to us with his hands clasped. "Tis Kevin!" says he like he'd say "Tis God!" and he pointed out this big blonde guy with a Take That haircut across his forehead an an enormous fuckin camera on his shouldur. There were guys draggin all kinds a equipment outa the van.

"What're they doin?" yelped Dec.

"Tis RTE. Kevin tought he'd take de opportunity, as he was comin down to see me like, to go down to Gougane Barra an do a documentary about St Finbarr so I told him about de funeral an dey were very interested so dey tought dey'd do Little Nellie too an de funeral an all because tis topical, see, because of de AIDS an all – "

"*Tizzy, yeh fuckin moron!*" yelled Liam with the cups clatterin in his fist. "*Me mothur doesn't even know we're havin this an now she's goin ta see it nation-wide on hur TV screen!* To say nothin a Cliona out sick from work an Niall on the lang from school an Fawlty ferryin geriatrics in the Squad car an Liz draggin Timmy up here an Drachma not wantin hur clients to know about the AIDS an – "

"Oh, I'm sorry, Liam," said poor Tizzy, gulpin as if he might cry. "I'm sorry, I'm sorry, I didn't tink a any a dat! I tought twould be great like – "

"What'm I goin to say to me mothur? What'm I goin to say? *You* didn't think! A course yeh didn't think with nothin but Bosco's dick up in yur brain! Shur how could yeh *think*! Well, I hope before the night is out he takes that fuckin camera an shoves it up yur ass!"

"Liam, Liam! Control yourself!" said Dec. "No profanity please! We're on holy ground. It seems we must resign ourselves to fame. Tizzy, don't forget in your excitement when you're being interviewed to mention that you've only got the one ball – "

"I told em dat already – "

"Oh, fine – then they can broadcast it to the nation."

The RTE people tore off to the graveyard at this point with Bosco behavin like he was leadin the final assault on the last occupied hill at Iwo Jima.

"Holy hour!" said Dec. "Tizzy, keep yer head down an don't step on a landmine."

Tizzy was lookin at him stupid. Dec had caught me thought like I'd thrown him a ball.

"Here, give Bosco a cup a tea. Milk, Liam!" Liam poured the milk, scowlin. "Are yeh seein him when he comes back from Gougane?"

"Oh, I'm goin with him – me bag's in the van –"

An off he went carryin his cups very carefully.

Dec struck a very camp pose with his kettle on his hip. "Well, honest to God! Liam? Could you imagine *anyone* fancyin Tizzy that much? Tis a mystury what turns people on! I don't understand it. But why am I talking to *you*? *You're* the pervert who's signed up for Mad Mary!"

"Well, somebody has to," said Liam.

"Why, in God's name?"

"Ah, shu' God help him!"

"You're feeling *sorry* for him? Well, *that's* a waste of time! Shur he's got no more feelings than a-a-a *parrot*! I don't understand you, Liam!"

Liam gave a shrug. "I might do worse."

"Don't *delude* yourself! You couldn't do worse if you scoured the sewers!"

"Ah, shur, tis a bit a craic like!"

Dec stared an gave a little shake a the head. "But c'mere – I'm curious. Tell me before we go in – what's it actually like to fuck with that creature?"

"Well," says Liam, scuffin with the toe of his shoe at the doorstep an considerin his answur. "Tis a bit like fuckin a particularly bony hen –"

He looked Dec straight in the eye.

"I can well imagine," says Dec. Sniff.

"But y'know," says Liam slowly. "I've heard it said that that's not an experience to be passed up –"

The two a them burst out laughin. I wanted to laugh meself but, to tell yeh the truth, I was feelin very faint. An worse by the minute.

Was I dyin? This wasn't fair! I'd already died once! Why should I havta do it again? In they went.

It looks like freedom but it feels like death

It's somethin in between I guess

The corridors, the kitchen an meself among the tea-caddies.

In comes the Bride an Ursula lookin for the lads.

"You never told us you were bringing RTE," said the Bride, very reproachful. "I don't know what the bishop will say. We really should have his permission."

"Oh, we didn't know, Mothur," said Dec. "We were shocked ourselves. We had no idea!"

"I think the bishop won't be pleased," said the Bride. "And really we should have asked his permission in the first place – for the funeral itself. I didn't realise it would be such an event!"

"You're a bold bold boy, Liam," said Ursula, slappin the back a his hand.

"And really, I'm not at all sure about the official position on cremation you know," said the Bride. "Perhaps the old ruling has only been rescinded in Australia –"

This was hardly the moment for Dec to do what he next did. But all I can say is twas absolutely typical a him. I think he would a done it even if there was no chance a Bosco an Co. broadcastin it to the nation. I'd say he intended to do it all the time. I dunno why – tis just *him*.

He put down the kettle. Oh, the blessed relief!

"There's something I have to tell ye, Mothur." Very low an precise. I knew the tone an that it always meant somethin hair-raisin.

"Ye-es? What is it?" crackled the Bride.

Two pairs a eyes – no, three includin Liam – fixed on him.

"It's about the circumstances of his death."

"Suicide!" said the Bride, fearin the worst. "Heavens! How am I going to tell the bishop!"

"Oh, no, Mothur! He actually died of AIDS."

The Bride tried to dislocate hur jaw again. "Ooh?"

Ursula's rosy face went pale. She bit hur lip with hur big white teeth.

"Did you hear that, Ursula?" said the Bride, swivellin hur eyes to Ursula without lettin go of the death-grip on hur own jaw. Maybe I might get lucky – she might call off the funeral.

"Yes, I did, Mother," said Ursula in a kinda whispur.

The Bride stared at Ursula from undur her brows an then swivelled an stared at Dec. An back again to Ursula.

"The bishop won't like this," says she.

"It's a pity we didn't know, Mother," said Ursula.

"I thought it would be only fair to tell ye," said Dec, very firm.

I've nevur seen Liam look so anxious. He was starin at the Bride like she was goin to prophesy.

"Well, I don't know what we can do about it now," said the Bride through hur nose, lettin go of hur jaw. "Do you, Mother Ursula?" An out came the handkurchief an the throat-clearin began. I raised the Magnum 45. I had me strength back by this time.

"No, Mother," said Ursula. "If we had asked the bishop's permission – but tis too late now –"

"Yes, indeed, but who would have expected RTE? Well, I'm afraid it's a case of being killed for a sheep rather than a lamb –"

An with that she spat into hur handkurchief an I blew hur away. An as sure as I did, whether twas the jolt or what, I was jolted back into the tea-caddy – I mean the urun – all a me togethur again.

Alive an kickin so to speak.

"Well, the chaplain should be ready,' said the Bride. "Though what kind of hand he'll make of it, Ursula, I don't know, with no preparation."

An out they all went.

An there I sat.

Me mind was clear again. But desperate.

Shur they mightn't miss me at all in the confusion. They might go through the whole funeral without me. I might sit here for the rest a me afturlife or at least till the Magdalens consumed me for elevenses.

I imagined what was goin on outside. "Give's the urun!" "I don't have it!" "Yes, you do!" "No, I don't! I thought you had it!" "You had it last!" "Jaysis, we've lost it!" "We musta left it in O'Brien's!"

They might *nevur* find me here.

And I swear it happened just like this –

I wanted to see Dec for one last time.

But if I stayed here maybe I could stay – alive? It mightn't be the end – if I wasn't scattured like. The Magdalens mightn't evur drink me. No, they'd use me for cleanin the range.

But anyway I didn't want any afturlife sittin in a convent kitchen nevur seein Dec or the othurs.

Bettur be scattured an go out with a blast.

– busted in the blindin lights

Of closin time –

It seemed a long time before they came an found me.

Then down the cold corridors like the prisonur bein escorted from his cell. Death Row. Mary, Queen a Scots. What was all that stuff again? Dec? Mary, Queen a Scots?

An I heard the words runnin through his brain clear as a bell: You do me a great good in withdrawing me from this world out of which I am glad to go –

But I don't feel like that at all, Dec! I'm not glad to go! I love bein here!

Up the hill at the side a the convent we went with the sudden sunshine blindin me eyes.

– busted in the blindin light –

An there was the grave an they were all gathured round an the camera people were clamberin all ovur the place an half the people there were tryin to hide their faces from the cameras.

There was the mosaic that caused all the trouble an the Infant a Prague with his crown an The Whole Woruld in His Hand – his one ball like Tizzy's – an some wreaths an flowurs.

So what now? Would I melt into the spirit a four-year-old Little Nellie? Would I meet hur? Was she still around?

An there was One Flew Ovur lyin Mary's bear out in the grave like a cot an Liz an the Bonny Boy an Mike all tryin to humour him. How the fuck did they manage to separate Mary from the bear?

An Godilmighty, was that the priest? He was the most decrepit thing I'd evur seen on two legs – talk about dodderin! They shoulda stuck to Breeda.

Yeah! Woman priests! I'm all for it! An married priests too! Let's just say yes to everythin – we've bein sayin no long enough for all the good it's done us.

The priest cleared his throat. They started sayin the Rosary.

The First Glorious Mystery: Jesus is raised from the dead.

I'm stubborn as those garbage bags

That time cannot decay –

Mrs Leary was cryin – snifflin away. Drachma was cryin an hur mascara was runnin down her cheeks.

One Flew Ovur was tryin to eat a wreath.

The Second Glorious Mystery: Jesus ascends into Heaven.

I'm junk but I'm still holdin up

This little wild bouquet –

The Third Glorious Mystery: the Descent of the Holy Spirit.

Breeda was leadin the prayurs. The voices ran through the Hail Marys like waves comin an goin on the shore.

It's comin from the women and the men

Oh baby, we'll be makin love again

We'll be goin down so deep

That the river's goin to weep

And the mountain's goin to shout Amen!

The Fourth Glorious Mystery: the Assumption of Our Lady into Heaven.

Remember O Most Gracious Virgin Mary –

Well, thank you for all the happy endings. But
rembur what I asked you about Dec? You haven't
forgotten that?

The Fifth Glorious Mystery: the Crowning of Our Lady
in Heaven.

Dec was leadin.

Every heart to love will come
But like a refugee –

A silence.

"Dearly beloved," croaked the priest. "We are gathered
here together –"

To get through this thing called life!

I'd a liked to have Prince sing at me funeral.

The priest was kinda swayin from side to side like he
might topple ovur. He was havin terrible trouble with this
frog in his throat an had to harrumph between every
sentence. He musta been related to the Bride.

" – so today we thank God for the life of – ah, ah, ah,
our friend – we trust that God will forgive him whatever
sins he may have committed –"

I don't claim to be guilty
Guilty's too grand –

An how about me forgivin God?

" – and we return this faithful servant to his master –
hah, hah, hah, *harrumph*! And we must feel no resentment
– we must say with Augustine: Thou hast made us for
Thyself, O Lord, and our hearts are ever restless till they
rest in Thee – hah, hah, hah, harrumph!"

But if my spirit is strong
I know it can't be long
No question I'm not alone
Somehow I'll find my way home –

Breeda stepped forward.

Yes, Breeda? I want to hear what you have to say.

"Just a few words. I'll speak for myself, not for

everybody here. Because we all had our own view of
Tony, I suppose, our own way of seeing him. So for me –
maybe because I'm in the business – I saw him as a very
spiritual person –"

A truer word you nevur said, Breeda.

"I saw him as someone who was always searching and
learning. Maybe his search was for love and we can be
sure he has found that at last. I like to think his search was
for God."

I loved you for your body
There's a voice that sounds like God to me
Declarin – Declarin
Declarin that your body's really
Really really you –

So then they scattured me. I think they were all
confused with the ordinary funeral where people throw
clods a earth on the coffin, y'know? Because they all had a
go (somebody should a brought a spoon): some of em just
took a pinch like a pinch a salt, othurs of em goin in for
handfuls. One Flew Ovur had to be restrained from eatin
his handful – they should a let him.

Now they were nearly all weepin – an again they all
had their own style – with Cliona, Tizzy, Drachma, Mary
an Liam goin for the Oscurs in that ordur. But Uncle Ned
was puttin in a good effort too an Mrs O'Leary an Mike an
Liz.

Dec didn't shed a tear. Just scattured away like the
Anjul a Death.

I didn't feel any different aftur bein scattured – still bein
all present an correct an that includes the bits consumed by
the company. Twas a bit ticklish like – like a crawlin across
yur scalp, y'know?

You mighta thought that was the end but not at all!
Cliona musta felt the othurs were stealin the show – that I
was stealin the show – an that wouldn't do our Cliona! Oh

no, not by a long shot! So she stepped ovur to the headstone with the Infant a Prague on top a it an leaned against it with one arm around the base a the Infant.

Oh, Jesus, I thought, I don't deserve this! Then she flung back the veil of hur hat an raised hur tear-streaked face to the sky. She held this pose till she was sure she had everyone's attention an all the cameras were focused on hur an then she opened hur big horse's mouth an burst inta song.

She has a grand voice, I must admit – an amazin powurful low rich voice.

Swing low, sweet chariot,
Comin for to carry me home!

They all started joinin in with the refrain:

Comin for to carry me home!

Cliona sang:

I looked over Jordan
And what did I see?

An they all went:

Comin for to carry me home!

An Cliona went:

Swing low, sweet chario-ot

All:

Comin for to carry me home!

Cliona:

I looked over Jordan –

Anyway, twas when she was lookin out ovur Jordan for the fifth time that it dawned on me: the bitch had forgotten the words an was just repeatin hurself. Nobody else knew the words eithur.

Jesus Christ Almighty, isn't this awful altogethur, I thought. Couldn't they stick to *Nearur My God to Thee*?

Cliona solved hur problem like the troopur she is: she broke down. She swayed against the Infant an colossal sobs broke outa hur. Fawlty it was who stepped forward an led hur off to the side with hur weepin on his manly chest.

Which left the othurs battlin on with the Sweet Chariot.

Comin for to carry me home!
Swing low sweet chario-ot
Comin for to carry me home!
You an me we sweat an strain
Comin for to carry me home!
Body all achin and racked with pain
Comin for to carry me home!
Tote that bar and lift that bale
Comin for to carry me home!

What the fuck was goin on?

Get a little drunk and you land in jail
Comin for to carry me home!

Mothur had started to laugh. Uncle Ned was gigglin. Breeda's eyes were opened wide an she had hur fingurs to hur mouth.

I get weary an sick of tryin
Comin for to carry me home!
An tired of livin an scared a dyin
Comin for to carry me home!

Mothur an Uncle Ned stopped laughin an joined in with a will for the grand finale.

But Old Man Rivur he just keeps rollin
He keeps on rollin
A-a-a-a-long!

For fuck's sake!

I had to laugh though.

So that was it. I was still there in me scattured ashes. As stubborn as those garbage bags that time cannot decay.

"A right balls we made a that!" said Dec in disgust as the funeral broke up an swarmed down the side a the convent to the trestle-tables an the sandwiches. "Jesus, I need a drink! C'mon an we nip down to the pub on the cornur an have a couple a quick ones – we'd be back before they notice."

"Hould yur horses now," said Liam. "We've waited all day for those sandwiches."

"I'm on a fast."

"Balls to yur fast! I'm hungry."

So we made off down the hill to the sandwiches.

Liam started stuffin his face immediately.

"Very nice, the whole affair," said the Bride in our ear, totally through the nose. "And such a lovely group of people. I had such an interesting chat with that nice man with the beard. The artist. He said he might do a mural in the chapel for us."

"Denis?" said Dec. "Oh, he'd do a lovely job for you!"

"A bachelor, I believe?" Through the nose.

"Yes," said Dec.

"Such a shame – he'd make a lovely family man."

"Oh, I believe he's considering it," said Dec.

"Oh, he should! And does he have someone in mind?"

"Oh, yes – he's had his eye on someone for a few years now."

"Lovely! I think there's nothing like family life, don't you agree?"

"Absolutely," said Dec. Liam (who had his mouth full of sandwich an was swiggin back tea) nodded like mad.

"Which reminds me – I had a chat with that nice girl – where is she?" The Bride scanned the crowd. "In fact, I've offered her a job in the laundry. We don't have enough Magdalens these days to keep it going, you know."

"In the *laundry*? Who? Drachma?"

"Drachma? You know I don't know her name –"

"She probably means Cliona," put in Liam.

"Oh, Mothur, I *hope* you don't mean the girl who sang *Swing Low, Sweet Chariot*?"

"No, no," said the Bride, vexed. "The girl who brought

the teddy-bear for that poor afflicted boy – the girl in the black dress – "

Liam spluttured his sandwich an tea all ovur the place.

"She told me she's engaged and wants to save up to get married," said the Bride. Then she did a bit of a double take at Liam. "But what am I talking about? Aren't you her boyfriend?"

Liam started to choke an had to be belted on the back by Dec.

"You know," said the Bride, very confidential. She seemed to be takin Liam an Dec as great pals at this stage. "I'm hoping the bishop will look on all of this as welcome publicity for the convent. I mean we could do with a little more income and I think something could be made from Little Nellie – "

"'Tis an ill wind, Mothur, that nevur did nobody no good," said Dec.

"And in any case we really had no control over the situation – about the TV programme I mean."

"Ah, shur, Mothur," said Dec. "You can always say: twould happen to a bishop!"

"Ah hah hah haaaaah!" went the Bride an hit Dec a ferocious belt between the shouldur-blades.

Ovur came Ursula at a trot – all excitement. "Mother!" she gasped, breathless. "They want permission to go inside and film Little Nellie's room!"

Off strode the Bride with a gleam in hur eye.

Wild horses couldn't have got Liam away from the sandwiches.

Dec grabbed up a plate a sandwiches to do his caterin act again an made for his mothur on the far side a the crowd.

Mrs O'Leary was lookin very pretty, all flushed from the tea an the excitement, in hur pink hat. She was talkin to Sistur Breeda.

"Listen, Mam," says Dec, drawin the two a them inta a huddle. "This whole thing was organised by your daughtur Sistur Veronica, an Tony an Liam are our cousins, and she had to leave suddenly this mornin – for Australia. Hur Reverend Mothur committed suicide yesturday because of a drink problem – have yeh got all that?"

For answur his mothur twisted hur mouth an narrowed hur eyes. Breeda was grinnin mad.

"Did Sistur Veronica actually come up here?" Breeda wanted to know. "Or did she do the job by phone?"

"Oh, she visited the convent of course," said Dec.

"'Tis a pity she missed the funeral," said his mothur, very smart.

"Oh, she's here in spirit," says Dec.

An on we went with our sandwiches, caterin all the way an chattin to everybody.

It was while we were posin with two nuns bein filumed by one a Bosco the Rapist's minions – Dec with the plate a sandwiches in one hand an a heart-shaped wreath propped up on the othur arm – that me heart started to race.

I was just wonderin whethur I would come out in the photo peerin ovur Dec's left shouldur like his Guardian Anjul – like them photos a seances – when it hit me like a clap a thundur or a stroke a lightnin or a ton a bricks or somethin heavy an sudden an hair-raisin anyway.

How *could* I be peerin ovur Dec's left shouldur?

We were miles from the grave.

"Dec boy," says I, real breathless, as soon as he was free to listen. "I want to go ovur there to have a word with Mothur."

We went. I didn't have anythin to say to Mothur when we got there. I couldn't have spoken anyway – me heart was in me throat. I just stared at Mike, who was feedin One Flew Ovur with pieces a sandwiches, like I was in some kinda time-warp an was waitin to come outa it.

195

"Nice job, daaahling!" said Mothur. "I somehow feel we have laid poor dear Tony's spirit to rest at last, don't you?"

When we finally got back to Liam he was still eatin sandwiches – but with one hand. With the othur he was strokin Mary's bony backside – an not a squawk outa hur.

"I'm headin off," said Dec. "Are ye comin?"

Liam gulped down the sandwich. "We misewell," says he, speakin for himself an Mary both it seemed, an no wondur seein the way she was clung to him. He looked at Mary with an expression I wasn't useta seein on his face. I dunno – gentle. "What about yur bear?"

"Tis alright – Liz'll bring iss for me."

Dec started down the drive. I stayed where I was an watched him go. The sun was shinin on the blonde hair.

He swung round.

"Come on so," he said.

So I went with him like.